2α3

"*Get out of my room, damn you!*"

"You were not always so unwelcoming, Charlotte." The velvet, sexily accented softness of his voice, the way he said her name, confused her emotions, jumbling them up until she didn't know whether she was on her head or her heels, and through that turmoil grew the need to retaliate, to hurt him.

"I didn't welcome you. I just put up with you. There is a difference."

DIANA HAMILTON is a true romantic and fell in love with her husband at first sight. They still live in the fairy-tale Tudor house where they raised their three children. Now the idyll is shared with eight rescued cats and a puppy. But despite an often chaotic life-style, ever since she learned to read and write Diana has had her nose in a book—either reading or writing one—and plans to go on doing just that for a very long time to come.

Books by Diana Hamilton

Don't miss any of our special offers. Write to us at the following address for information on our newest releases.

Harlequin Reader Service
U.S.: 3010 Walden Ave., P.O. Box 1325, Buffalo, NY 14269
Canadian: P.O. Box 609, Fort Erie, Ont. L2A 5X3

DIANA HAMILTON

The Last Illusion

Harlequin Books

TORONTO • NEW YORK • LONDON
AMSTERDAM • PARIS • SYDNEY • HAMBURG
STOCKHOLM • ATHENS • TOKYO • MILAN
MADRID • WARSAW • BUDAPEST • AUCKLAND

ISBN 0-373-11716-7

THE LAST ILLUSION

CHAPTER ONE

CHARLEY paid the driver off at Plaza San Francisco. He had the grey eyes of a Berber in a face like a walnut, and they crinkled appreciatively as she added a generous amount of pesetas to the fare, thanking him in his own language.

At least her Spanish hadn't emerged too rustily, though Olivia, who had prided herself on her pure Castilian, would no doubt still deride the distinctive Andaluz dialect she had picked up from her teacher, Andrés, who had tended the sumptuous gardens behind Sebastian's town house here in Cadiz.

Despite the heat, a convulsive shudder rocked her too slender frame. She had no illusions. Olivia would spend as much time here as she had done before. Probably more. Facing her again, knowing what she knew, would be as hard, if not harder, than facing her husband.

Not that she had thought of Sebastian Machado as her husband since she had left him four years ago, she reminded herself as she picked up the small, soft-backed suitcase which had doubled as hand luggage on the flight from London to Jerez. She had cut him out of her life and, with a great deal of input from her aunt Freda, had made herself over, made a career of sorts for herself. And deciding, at last, to accept Gregory's offer of marriage had been the final and decisive change, a change that had irretrievably cancelled out the trauma of the past.

The only thing left to do was to ask Sebastian to agree to a divorce.

And to buy back those shares. Greg had told her to insist on that, though to her way of thinking nothing was as important as her legal freedom, certainly not the extra money, useful though it would be.

Restlessly her tawny eyes ranged around the pretty square as she wondered whether to give in to the cowardly temptation to sit at a table beneath the shade of one of the dozens of orange trees and sip at an ice-cold *jugo de naranja*, but decided against, because she knew her churning stomach would instantly reject anything she tried to put into it—even something as innocuous and refreshing as orange juice.

Besides, she had already allowed herself the concession of stopping off at the square, using the five minutes or so it would take to find her way on foot to the home she had once shared—with equal measures of rapture and pain—with Sebastian. Time enough to quell the unlooked-for flutter of nerves that was, dismayingly, threatening to turn into a full-scale attack.

Striking off into the narrow, shadowed streets of the old quarter, she tightened her jaw, ignoring the trickle of perspiration between her shoulderblades. Here, deep in the maze of narrow white streets, glinting with *miradores*—the glazed balconies that offered protection from the Atlantic breezes—she felt drainingly homesick. She had forgotten how much she had learned to love this joyous, bustling white city, built on the tip of a headland, thrusting so confidently out into the sea.

There was so much she had believed forgotten, both the good and the bad thrust willy-nilly into the dark netherworld of her soul where they could no longer hurt her. And when she caught her first glimpse of the ornate iron gates that seemed to overpower the narrow street she almost turned tail and ran, beginning to wish she had followed Greg's advice and done everything through her solicitor.

But she conquered the impulse as she had learned to conquer all her fears during the last four years. Beneath the sleekly styled ochre linen suit she had chosen to travel in, her slender body tautened with determination. It was just a house. Rather more splendid than most, but nevertheless just a house. Beyond the intricately fashioned gates lay a courtyard and beyond that the ancient, arcaded stone house, beyond that the gardens where the magnolia trees grew and within, somewhere among the dozens of sumptuous rooms, a place where she could quietly sit and collect herself until her husband returned from his arrogant office block in the commercial area beyond the ancient Moorish walls of the town.

And Teresa would bring her some tea.

Inconceivable that her old Spanish friend would have given up her jealously guarded position as Sebastian's housekeeper. Four years ago Teresa had ruled the household with an iron fist in a very threadbare velvet glove, and that wouldn't have changed.

Teresa had the tongue of a scold and the heart of a lion, but she had taken the almost painfully innocent girl Charley had been when she'd arrived here to her vast bosom. She had been nineteen years old when Sebastian had brought her here as his bride—with the experience and outlook of a child of ten, as Freda had tartly pointed out.

But that was no longer the case, she reminded herself as she pushed at the impressive iron gates. A year of marriage had all but broken her, but with Freda's initial help she had put her life back together, wiped Sebastian and what he had done from her brain, and had emerged as a twenty-four-year-old woman who was nobody's fool.

Sebastian meant nothing to her now. She couldn't even be bothered to hate him for what he had done. So instead of feeling nervous she would concentrate on her achievement in travelling the road to complete self-recovery!

And when he returned this evening she would be waiting, would calmly state her business, and the moment she had obtained his agreement—and surely there would be no problem there—she would get herself back to the safe predictability of England and Greg and her work and quietly look forward to an autumn wedding.

Passing quickly through the scented courtyard, not giving the vibrant heat, the perfume of orange blossom and oleanders time to seduce her senses, she entered the huge dim hall, marble-paved and cool, the walls clad with dark, elaborately carved wood, the marble staircase a thing of almost ethereal beauty, soaring upwards like a pathway to heaven.

And hell, she reminded herself staunchly, her small face going stiff with the determination to block out the instinctive appeal this land, its architecture and its people had exerted on her in the past. It wouldn't happen again. She had learned that appearances could often be deceptive, that people could lie, silver tongues saying things they didn't mean.

Blinking, trying to get her eyes to readjust after the whiteness of the light outside, she absorbed the silence of the great house. Siesta time, so it wasn't to be wondered at, and, rather than disturb Teresa, she would find herself somewhere to wait.

Putting her case down against one of the walls, she straightened, her ears picking up the faint rustle of fabric, a sibilant drag of indrawn breath, and her narrowed eyes fastened on a shimmer of white movement and she was fixed to the spot, because her feet seemed to have rooted themselves to the pale cold marble, and Sebastian said thickly, 'So you return, at last.'

She hadn't expected to see him so soon; it put her at a disadvantage. Thick dark lashes drifted down, briefly closing him out. The white cambric shirt made his olive-toned skin and his cropped midnight hair even darker, his narrow black trousers emphasising his long-legged leanness, the whippy strength of the hard, wide shoulders and non-existent hips. She had forgotten the impact he made.

She should have remembered, been more prepared.

Forcing her tawny eyes open, she stared at him with a cool and desperate defiance. Looks counted for nothing, she told herself. The rare combination of sultry, hooded black eyes and a wide, unashamedly sensual mouth with the harsh asceticism of bleakly carved cheekbones and jawline and the arrogant, aquiline cast of his nose had swept her giddily gullible head off her shoulders when they had first met five years ago.

But she saw more clearly now; he had the face of a fallen angel, the face of a man who could cold-bloodedly kill his own brother, who could pluck an innocent out of her own sheltered element, expose her to the dark pride and passion that was uniquely his own, use her, and betray her without blinking one of his own long, silky black lashes!

'For about half an hour,' she made herself answer, trying not to flinch as he stalked closer, like a black panther. 'It shouldn't take longer.'

'I am honoured.' His dark, intriguingly accented voice seemed to curl around her, and she shuddered. He smiled faintly. 'You go to the expense and trouble to leave your nest in the middle of England—Stanton Bottom, such a curious name—to fly out to spend a mere half-hour in my company. An honour indeed.'

'How did you know where I was?' Shock and dismay had her blurting the words out without thinking, and she watched his sensual mouth go thin, heard a vein of ice creep into his voice.

'If you imagine I would let you walk away from me and disappear, then you don't know me. But then——' the brooding black eyes hardened to glinting jet, '—past events adequately proved that you know more about the hidden side of the moon than you know about me. Isn't that so, *mi esposa*?' He spread one hand almost contemptuously, laying out the details of the last four years of her life as if they were beneath notice. 'You spent six months with your aunt in Harrow. She put you through a crash course and made sure you caught up with your abandoned business studies. She then packed you off to that place with the curious name in your English Midlands, where you worked as an assistant to the manager of a hotel-conference-centre-leisure park. Is that not so?'

'You spied on me!' Charley felt what little colour she had drain out of her face. She had thought she was safe, that as far as he was concerned she had disappeared off the face of the earth.

She shifted restlessly from one foot to the other, her teeth biting into her soft lower lip. All that time—the six months of sheer hard grind that had earned her the qualifications she needed, the job Aunt Freda had found through her business and domestic agency, tucked away on the edge of the Staffordshire moorlands. She had felt safe there, had been able to come to terms with what Sebastian had done, had grown in confidence and independence. And all the time he had known exactly where she was, what she was doing. It didn't bear thinking about. People must feel like this when they came home and found the house burgled and ransacked, their private possessions spewed around like so much tawdry, worthless debris.

'I prefer to think of it as keeping a watch over my own,' Sebastian stated, his aristocratically cut nostrils flaring with displeasure at her choice of words. The accusation of something as underhand as spying would not fit in with his exalted opinions of himself. He liked to think of himself as a man of honour—and woe betide anyone who had the temerity to impugn it—and didn't allow himself to understand that he had long ago compromised what honour he might once have had.

And the fact that he had kept tabs on her meant that he must know about Gregory Wilson, how they had met and how often they had dated. So at least her request for a divorce wouldn't come as a surprise, she thought, trying to feel tough.

But it was difficult to feel tough and in control of the situation when his lancing eyes informed her that he knew all there was to know about her and wasn't impressed.

'If we are to spend half an hour together, then I suggest we do it in comfort.' The drawled sarcasm turned her stomach, fiery little spirals igniting inside her as he took her arm and led her through to a small *sala* tucked away at the rear of the house. Being close to him, touched by him, made every nerve end quiver, forcing her to remember how just one sultry glance from those impenetrable black eyes had once had the power to reduce her to a mass of desperate, wanton needs.

It was a memory she refused to entertain and she shook her head as if to clear it, obeyed the slight movement of his hand and sat on a damask-covered chair, her spine rigid. And all around her the cool green light that filtered through the louvres touched the graceful Spanish renaissance furnishings, giving the heavily carved or richly painted pieces an air of soft mystery that would be lost in the full glare of sunlight. This was the room she had made her own, often coming here to read or simply to try to relax, especially when Olivia—with all that false friendliness—had been in residence.

Had Sebastian remembered? Had he chosen this room from the almost countless others because he knew it would give her pain? He must know that it had been here that Olivia had finally shed her veneer of matiness and spat out the cruel, devastating truth.

Charley straightened her already rigid shoulders and wished he'd sit down, but couldn't ask him to because to do so would reveal that his endless pacing, slow circling, was getting to her. She didn't want him to know that he could affect her on any level. And the way he moved with the insolent grace born of a natural arrogance, touched a long-forgotten core of unwanted female responsiveness deep within her.

'You have changed, Charlotte,' he pronounced at last.

The deep timbre of his voice, that wickedly sensual accent, flicked her on the raw and made her snap without thinking of what she might be revealing. 'I prefer Charley.' Only her parents, and Sebastian, had used her full name. She had loved her parents and now they were dead. She had loved Sebastian and, as far as she was concerned, he might as well be dead, too. She didn't want to be reminded.

'I refuse to call you by a name that would be ugly for a male and unthinkable for a female, especially a female who has grown into something quite remarkably sophisticated.'

The level look beneath lowered brows was tinged with an amused derision, she noted fumingly, as he lowered himself gracefully on to a velvet-covered *chaise*. If he had thought of her at all during the past four years it would have been as the slightly plump, wide-eyed nineteen-year-old he had married. Her mouse-brown hair had hung limply halfway down her back, and the only make-up she had used had been a smear of pale pink lipstick.

But she had lost a lot of weight after she'd left him and had never regained it, and her hair had darkened to a glossy seal-brown and she now wore it cut fashionably short. Freda had been initially responsible for the change in her style of dressing. Her, 'You can't go through life looking like Alice in Wonderland, not if you want to land a responsible, reasonably paid job. I loved my sister dearly, but she had a blind spot when it came to your upbringing. She insisted on dressing you like the Sugar Plum Fairy since the day you were born, and you couldn't have been more sheltered if you and your parents had lived out your lives as the sole inhabitants of a desert island,' had hurt at the time.

However, it hadn't taken too much soul-searching to acknowledge that Freda had been right. As the only child of parents who had feared that after fifteen years of marriage they would never have children, she had been too protected and sheltered.

Her education had been at a private, girls-only school, her friends carefully vetted, her out-of-school activities more suited to a Victorian miss than a girl of the twentieth century.

Her wish to take a business studies course and stay on in England when her parents retired to Spain had been granted only after endless and minute discussions. Only when her mother's younger, unmarried sister, Freda, had stepped in and offered to have her stay at her flat in Harrow had her wish been granted.

And even during that year Freda hadn't made more than a few half-hearted efforts to push her into the real world. While Charley's parents had been alive Freda hadn't felt able to interfere with the lifestyle of her quiet, studious and painfully innocent niece. Besides, she had been too engrossed in running her own successful agency to spare the effort needed to try to change someone who had been patently happy with the way she was.

But the way she had been then meant that she had been completely gullible, quite unable to see through a man like Sebastian Machado. A few kind words, a few careless caresses, had been enough to turn her silly, innocent head. No, he had needed to expend very little effort to ensure he got what he wanted: a woman who was stupid enough, besotted enough, to play the part he had allotted her in his devilish plans.

'Yes, I have changed.' She agreed, stony-voice, with his earlier statement and crossed her long, elegantly slender legs with a whisper of honey-toned silk, knowing that the fashionable short skirt of the suit she wore, her slender high heels, showed them off to advantage.

And strangely, the defiant little movement excited her, because there was a quiet assessment in the way he watched her, in the slide of those sultry eyes as they roamed down to the tips of her toes and back up again to her glinting eyes, and it told her his words hadn't been empty, that he acknowledged the change and accepted it. And that worked to her advantage.

As long as he realised that she was no longer the adoring little doormat who had been willing to submit to the hurts and humiliations he and his mistress, Olivia, had subjected her to for the sake of the meaningless caresses and empty words he deigned to spare her, then they could discuss terms as equals.

That alone would be worth the expense of this trip, the arguments she'd had with Greg when she'd told him of her decision to face her unwanted husband in person. At last she was the redoubtable Sebastian Machado's equal, and she had nothing whatever to fear!

Quickly, before his brooding presence made her change her mind on that score, she folded her hands tightly in her lap and told him crisply. 'I want a divorce.'

'Why?' His expression didn't alter by as much as a flicker of an eyelid. He brought his hands up, steepling his long, strong-boned fingers, the tips resting against the sweeping curve of his upper lip.

His cool question almost took her breath away, an insult in itself, and anger stirred, making her voice taut as she shot back, 'Need you really ask? Our marriage ended four years ago. It's high time we tidied up the loose ends.'

'And you think a divorce would get rid of those loose ends, extinguish the past? Are you that naïve?' His tone was still uninterested, the hooded eyes never leaving her face as he dropped in, 'You could have asked me for a divorce at any time during the past four years, or at least made your intention to seek one plain to me and my solicitor. Why didn't you, if our marriage had become so intolerable to you?'

That floored her. Charley felt her eyes go wide, staring into the dark and sultry depths of his as if she might find the answer there. During the past four years she had never tried to hide her married status, but she had never spoken of it to anyone except Freda and, much later, Greg. And even then she hadn't told all the truth, merely explaining that she and Sebastian had had irreconcilable differences. Divorce hadn't entered her head until Greg had proposed.

And she didn't know why. But she wasn't going to confess the sudden bewilderment his query had produced, because that might suggest she had clung on to the legality of their relationship because she couldn't face the final severance.

She closed her eyes briefly, and when she opened them again they glinted with cold amber lights. She could never inflict on him the type of pain he had dished out to her, but she could have the satisfaction of pricking his overblown ego a little. And her voice was tart as she informed him, 'You know why I left you. Do you imagine I wanted to remember you and what you had done?' Carefully, she unfurled the fingers she hadn't realised had been so tightly clenched and made herself rest her hands lightly on the slender carved wood arms of her chair. 'I blocked you, and our marriage, out of my mind. I never gave it a second thought until I realised I needed my freedom to marry again.'

She thought she had earned herself a reaction in the sudden spasm of a muscle along his hard jaw, but couldn't be sure. The tips of his fingers were still resting against his mouth, so she could have imagined it. She got to her feet, suddenly tired. She didn't have time to play games. The sooner this interview was over the sooner she could book into the modest hotel where she had reserved a room for the night.

His eyes swept up, lazily following her movement, his attitude still sublimely relaxed. And she said, 'As we haven't lived together for so long, I can't see how there can be any difficulties. Especially as ours was a civil wedding.' Olivia had spelled out exactly why that had been, why Sebastian had chosen not to have a religious ceremony, and Charley tacked on tightly, 'Greg and I would like to marry before the end of the year—in the autumn, preferably. Which gives us time, I would imagine, to get the divorce finalised.'

Suddenly, she needed to get out of here. It was as if the atmosphere of this house, the watchful presence of the man who had once meant more than life itself to her, was suffocating her, gathering her back into the web of deceit and cruelty, the binding strands interfaced with the wild magic of Andalucía, with the dark, irresistible charm of this devil in human guise that had almost broken her all that time ago.

She wouldn't even mention the possibility of his buying back those shares. That could be done later, through solicitors. She couldn't bring herself to spend one more moment with him. And she began to walk out of the room, making herself move slowly, because if she once gave in to the urgent desire to hurry she would find herself running until her lungs burst inside her.

'No.'

The single word lowered the temperature in the room by a thousand degrees, and Charley's feet felt as if they had been nailed to the floor as the blood in her veins turned to ice. But he couldn't possibly mean what she thought he meant, she berated herself, then swung round quickly, defensively, because she could hear him moving, coming towards her.

'Under Spanish law a divorce is possible if the couple have been living apart for two years—provided, of course, that both are agreed.' His black eyes mocked her. 'Unless the desire for a divorce is mutual, then the statutory period of separation is five years.'

He smiled for the first time, but it didn't touch his eyes. It was a mere baring of teeth that sent icy trickles of disbelief running down her spine.

'You can't be serious!' Her voice emerged thickly and she had no control over the flood of dismay that sent hectic colour to stain her cheeks. She stepped back, her poise deserting her. He was crowding her, much too close, making her achingly aware of the scent of him, the warmth of him, the shockingly vibrant, power-packed, raw masculinity of him.

'Never more so.' His voice was an assured purr, and it made her stomach churn.

She was backed against the impenetrability of one of the walls, but he didn't move closer. If he had done, their bodies would have been touching, but he didn't need to make such an open statement of his physical domination, because already she felt weak and giddy, as if she were about to faint for the first time in her life.

There were tiny dancing lights in the brooding blackness of his eyes, and the graceful, upward lilt of one arched black brow reinforced his wicked amusement, the machiavellian satisfaction he derived from gaining the upper hand.

'So, *mi esposa*, you have another full year to wait before you can even begin divorce proceedings.'

He placed his palms flat against the wall, on either side of her head, and she was trapped, and frightened, yet determined not to show it. And she told him fiercely, 'Call yourself a man? You're nothing but a spiteful little worm!' and had the satisfaction of seeing him stiffen, his proud features frozen over as he dropped his hands and stepped back, his shoulders high and hard.

'Explain yourself!' He looked as if he would like to kill her where she stood, and she didn't even care. She was beyond being frightened, even by a man who had committed the ultimate crime—slaughtering his own brother for financial gain!

She hurled at him defiantly, 'What reason could you have for wanting to delay our divorce? You don't want me. You never did! But you don't want me to be happy with another man. That makes you spiteful!'

She sprang away from the wall, side-stepping him. Another year in an extinct marriage wouldn't mean a thing to him. Olivia was content to wait for just as long as it took; she had openly said as much. The two of them had been lovers for ages, well before he had conned her into hurtling into marriage, and they would be lovers as long as they both drew breath, whether or not Olivia bore his name and wore his ring! And she told him witheringly, making for the door again, 'Don't think a year's postponement of our marriage will make a scrap of difference to Greg and me. It won't.'

She was sure of that, at least. Greg was a pragmatic soul. He could be patient. But her cheeks went very hot when he tossed at her, almost idly, 'I am not in the least concerned about Gregory Wilson. He is no threat. He is, in fact, beneath notice.'

She glared at him hotly, her worst fears confirmed. She hadn't mentioned Greg's surname; his spies would have discovered that and reported back. So she'd been right when she'd half hysterically decided that he'd ferreted out every fact about her life, known precisely when she and Greg had met, how often they'd dated. It made her feel besmirched!

'If you want to marry a middle-aged small-town accountant with a pot belly, an aversion to parting with his money and a fixation on his mother, then I can only mourn your lowered standards. I can't prevent you, if such is your ultimate wish. But don't ask me to make it too easy for you.'

'Oooh!' Charley couldn't begin to express the disgust she felt. Her mind was reeling. How did he have the gall to accuse her of lowering her standards when he was the cruellest, most heartless, wickedest man she had ever had the misfortune to meet?

And Greg wasn't middle-aged! He was thirty-seven, a mere three years older than Sebastian. And he did *not* have a pot belly—he was cuddly! And if he was careful with his money it wasn't to be wondered at. His father had died before he'd left school, and his mother, with whom he'd continued to live until her death from a stroke almost a year ago, had had to scrimp and scrape to support him while he got his qualifications and even afterwards, while he struggled to get started up on his own. So it was little wonder he had been a devoted and grateful son, averse to throwing his hard-earned money around, because he had known what it was like to count every penny.

'At least he doesn't promise me the moon and stars wrapped up in gold ribbon,' she managed at last, hating him, 'then hand me something poisonous!'

'And what does he promise you?' His menacing body tensed, his mouth like a steel trap, his eyes boring into her head as he uttered, '*No importa!* It is of no consequence.' The hard, white-clad shoulders lifted imperceptibly, then he swung on his heels and pressed the bell push near the door. 'I have summoned Teresa. She will either show you to your room, or she will show you to the door. You have the choice.'

'I can find my own way out. I used to live here, remember?'

No way was she staying under this roof, even for one night. He had to be off his head even to suggest such a thing! But she knew his sanity was not in question, only the depths of his deviousness, as he told her softly, 'I am willing to meet you part way, Charlotte. Agree to stay here for four weeks, and if, at the end of that time, you still wish to marry your dumpy accountant, I will agree to a divorce and will ensure that all goes through as swiftly as possible. Go, and you wait a further year. And be warned, I am well able to make sure that the proceedings crawl along at less than a snail's pace. Believe me, I can make it happen.'

CHAPTER TWO

'HE WANTS you to do *what*?'

Greg sounded as if he couldn't believe his ears, and Charley gripped the receiver more tightly and repeated, 'Stay put for four weeks. If I do, he'll agree to the divorce. If I don't, he won't.' She lowered her voice, even though she was alone in the book-lined room Sebastian used as a study. 'We would have to wait another year before I could even start proceedings. I thought it was worth it,' she added quickly, although she wasn't too sure about that.

'What's he up to? Does he want a reconciliation?'

Greg's tone was suspicious, and she couldn't blame him. But the very idea was laughable, and she assured him, 'Of course not.' He had never wanted her, except as a body upon which to get an heir. When he'd claimed that he'd fallen in love with her, almost on sight, he'd been lying. Sebastian Machado was good at lying.

But there was no way she could reassure Greg, because she didn't know what lay behind her unwanted husband's stipulation. A downright refusal to agree to a divorce she could have understood and put down to spite. But his promised agreement after four weeks of her company was beyond her comprehension. Something devious and tricky, no doubt...

'Well, something's going on,' Greg said peevishly. 'When Glenda and I got our divorce there was no trouble. She walked out on me, and as there were no

23

children...' The word was bitten off and then he asked warily, 'You don't have children, do you?'

'Do you think I'd have kept it from you if I had?' Charley snapped. If there had been children, then Sebastian would have instigated divorce proceedings himself as soon as the mandatory two years had passed, and made good and sure he got custody—she would have been lucky to get even limited access! And she could understand Greg's unease about this turn of events, but he had no call to be suspicious where she was concerned!

'Of course not, darling,' he soothed. 'I'm sorry, but the whole thing looks suspect from where I'm standing. Are you sure that living with him again won't prejudice everything?'

It hadn't entered her head, and she bit her lip, frowning at the window-panes, which were reflecting the fiery descent of the sun. And she answered slowly, 'I don't think so. It isn't as if I'll be sharing his bed.' The very thought of sharing his bed made her whole body clench with a huge, painfully intense spasm which she quickly translated as revulsion, and, gathering herself, she went on quickly, if a little hoarsely, 'I'll phone my boss in the morning and explain the need for extra leave.'

'Dev won't like it.' Not any more than he did, Greg's sharp tone implied, but Charley silently excused him, because the circumstances were exceptional.

'He'll manage. There weren't any problems or upheavals on the horizon, and Dawn's very competent.' Dawn was the secretary she shared with Mark Devlin, the manager of the complex, and as she, Charley, had been Dev's personal assistant for over three years and never once used her full holiday entitlement she couldn't foresee any great problems where extra leave was concerned.

But it wasn't going to be her idea of a holiday, she thought as she said her goodbyes to the still disgruntled Greg and replaced the receiver, promising to keep in touch.

Her original intention had been to spend a week in Spain, leaving Cadiz first thing in the morning, having obtained Sebastian's agreement to a divorce, hiring a car, and taking the rest of the week to say her farewells to this exuberant, flamboyant, passionate yet hauntingly soulful corner of Andalucía.

Instead, she was being forced to squander her leave, staying here as a hostage to Sebastian's no doubt devious schemes, unable even to enjoy this beautiful city, because she would be on tenterhooks—wouldn't she just?—watching and waiting for the smallest clue to his diabolical intentions.

Her mood was self-admittedly foul as she walked out of the study into the gloom of the hall. The day was dying quickly, and rather than hang around, kicking her heels, she would run Teresa to earth in the kitchens. At least with her she knew exactly where she was. With Sebastian, she knew nothing!

The housekeeper's face had lit up with pleasure when she had answered Sebastian's summons and found Charley waiting, wooden-faced with distaste for the way she was being coerced into staying here. But Teresa's rapid-fire Spanish, half scolding, half welcome, soon brought a grin to her face as she pleaded in that language, 'Slow down! I'm rusty—I need more practice!'

'Then that I will give you—Andrés, too. He is still here—everyone is still here; all is the same as it was. All waiting for you to come home.'

It was only Sebastian's cool demand that the *señora's* room be made ready that stopped the flow, and that only after the stout elderly woman had imparted, 'All has been in readiness for four years, Don Sebastian, make no mistake. And now, perhaps, we will not see such a high head and such a long face!'

Recalling the look of smothered irritation on the dark devil's face, Charley relaxed her soft lips reluctantly into a smile. Teresa was no respecter of persons—no matter how exalted they believed themselves to be. In Charley's year-long experience of her rule, Teresa was never afraid to speak her mind, though she herself doubted if her enforced presence here would make much difference to Sebastian's 'high head and long face'! Unless it was a sly smile of satisfaction at having forced her, yet again, to dance to his tune.

Nevertheless, she might do well to emulate the housekeeper's bluntness where her unwanted husband was concerned. She might even be able to cut him down to size once in a while. Because, although she had given in to his demands on this one occasion, it wouldn't happen again. Four weeks here, under his roof, was as far as it would go!

She found Teresa in the kitchen, ordering Pilar— the maid-of-all-work—around in stentorian tones, and had her own offer of help rejected in the same decisive manner.

'The kitchen is not the place for you, *señora*. Tomorrow I will come to you for your instructions. Have you forgotten all I taught you?'

'Dare I ever?' Charley riposted drily, remembering with affection how immediately Teresa had sized up her lack of experience, had thrust her firmly beneath her wing and taught her all she needed to know about running a Spanish household of this size. And now the housekeeper seemed to think she had come back to stay, and at the moment she didn't have the heart or any real inclination to explain that she was only here for four weeks, and that under duress.

Charley left the room disconsolately, because helping with the preparations for the evening meal would have taken her mind off what she had let herself in for. And not knowing what exactly she had let herself in for, what Sebastian had had in mind when he had made his agreement to a divorce conditional upon her staying here, was going to give her night-mares. Already she had the beginnings of a niggling headache, and she guessed she ought to go to her room and try to relax. She would need to be on top form, have every last one of her wits about her, if she were to hold her own with him over dinner tonight, dem-onstrate that she wasn't the feeble push-over she'd been when he'd first met her.

To her quiet amazement she found her way through the passages as if she'd never been away, and laid the palm of her hand on the sumptuously carved door to her room as if she had only walked out of it an hour or so ago.

She had proudly believed that she'd forgotten everything, erased the year of her marriage—and all that had gone with it—right out of her mind. Now she knew that it wasn't in her power to forget, and quickly, before she panicked and blindly ran from the Casa de las Surtidores and the memories it contained, she pushed the door open and resolutely stepped inside.

The wide, long room was exactly as she had left it, she saw as she flicked the switch down and the lamps in their delicate holders sprang to glittering life along the length of the room.

Everything—the row of tall shuttered windows, the arch of the carved and painted ceiling, the ornate furniture and near-priceless carpet—everything, right down to the crystal vase of the long-stemmed white roses she had always used to pick from the garden to place on the table near the bed.

The lump in her throat made her grit her teeth. It was like stepping back in time, watching the hands of the clock of her life spin relentlessly backwards, like finding a part of herself she had presumed lost.

And she couldn't bring herself to look at the bed.

They'd had separate rooms, right from the start. She hadn't been able to understand it at first. It had been the first hurt he had inflicted. The first of many. Transplanted into this vibrant, alien land, surrounded by the undreamt-of elegance and luxury of old and arrogant wealth, by deferential servants whose language she couldn't understand, swept away from her quiet, studious background, from everything she was familiar with, she had been too unsure of herself to question the sleeping arrangements and had comforted herself by deciding that it must be a Spanish custom.

Of course he had visited her from time to time, his lithe body dominating her between the silken sheets, sweeping her away on an avalanche of rapture she hadn't known how to handle. But she had slept alone for many long, lonely nights, willing him to come to her, if only to hold her comfortably in his strong arms and sleep at her side, then gradually coming to understand the pattern, recognise how he never came near her when Olivia was in residence.

He hadn't needed to.

Only when the scalding of tears flooded her eyes did she take a firm grip on herself. This wouldn't do! Surely she had more self-respect than to weep for the slice of her past she had already consigned to a mental dustbin?

Jerking her chin up, she turned and looked at the bed and made herself see it for what it was: simply a superb piece of furniture, a great, voluptuous four-poster, the carvings depicting a riot of flowers and fruit and improbable cherubs, the whole thing swagged and swathed with fine jade-green silk.

At least she should get a good night's sleep, she told herself prosaically. If she remembered correctly, it was supremely comfortable. And of course everything remained the same—why shouldn't it? She doubted if much had been changed since the house had been built!

And as for the white roses—well, Teresa must have remembered how she had enjoyed cutting them herself from the gardens, under Andrés's watchful yet friendly eyes, how the small task had given her something to do, how she'd enjoyed the way the blooms had perfumed the room, the welcome sight of their pale purity comforting her a little when she emerged from her often bitter dreams.

And someone had deposited her case on the chest at the foot of the bed. Footsteps firm, she walked over and snapped open the catches. She had brought very little with her, just one or two cotton skirts and tops, a serviceable pair of washed-out jeans, a swimsuit and enough changes of underwear to last the week she had allowed herself.

So if Sebastian still dressed for dinner, tough. He would have to put up with her looking like the budget-class tourist she had planned on being, driving around the province, staying at low-cost hostels or restaurants with rooms, saying goodbye to the places she had grown to love, knowing she would never return.

Selecting a gathered skirt in fine black cotton and a sleeveless cream-coloured cotton top, she laid them on the bed and carried the rest of the things over to the cavernous wardrobe, and felt her heart clench with shock as she dragged open the heavy doors.

All the things she had left behind were still here: the silks, glistening satins, the froths of chiffon and the elegant severity of tailored linen and heavy sleek cotton. Charley stared at the expensive garments, her mouth going tight.

Sebastian had been generous with his money; she could never accuse him of stinginess. But then—her mouth went even tighter—being generous when he had enough to keep him in luxury for half a dozen lifetimes was hardly a big deal!

And she had been so lonely at times—lonely for his company—that she had forced herself to make treats for herself, enlisting the help of one of Teresa's many nieces, Francisca, arranging for her to accompany her to Seville—even Barcelona or Madrid—staying a few nights in luxurious hotels and buying everything in sight. But no matter how much she'd spent, how beautiful the clothes, she had still felt gauche when Olivia had been around.

Olivia had been so beautiful, so svelte and charming, that Charley had felt like a bunchy, over-dressed schoolgirl. So she'd given up trying to compete, had stopped spending Sebastian's money, and had concentrated fiercely on the language lessons she was having, mostly from Andrés as she pottered around with him as he worked in the gardens, but sometimes from Pilar, Teresa or Francisca—whoever could spare her the time.

She hadn't told Sebastian she was learning his language; that was to be her big surprise. Olivia was able to converse fluently—a necessity, she had once told Charley, her manner vaguely patronising. For although Cadiz had a longer history than any other city in the Western world it didn't turn itself inside out to attract foreign tourists. Cadiz stayed exactly as it was because that was the way the Gaditanos wanted it, and very few people spoke English. If you wanted to become accepted, do business with them, or socialise, then speaking the language was essential. The Gaditanos were full of defiant independence.

So Charley had beavered away, and as soon as she had been confident enough she had taken the conversational initiative over the dinner-table, sure that her achievement would be applauded, taken as a compliment, by her very own defiantly independent Gaditano.

But she hadn't properly thought it out. If she had done, she would have waited until Olivia was back in England, stamping around in her role of manager of the UK branch of the Machado import-export company. Because Olivia had raised one perfectly arched brow, her smile slightly withering as she'd commented, 'Well done. But what a deplorable accent! Who taught you? A *gitano*?'

Sternly ignoring the sudden ache in the region of her heart, Charley pushed the exquisite clothes as far as she could along the hanging rail to make room for the few bits and pieces she'd brought with her.

This room was having a bad effect on her, bringing back floods of unwanted memories. She was going to have to do something about it.

Beginning with getting rid of all those clothes. If Teresa didn't know someone who could make use of them, then Pilar or Francisca would. She wouldn't be using them herself. No way. Besides, she thought with a heartening quirk of her lips, nothing would fit.

Getting her act together wasn't so difficult, was it? she chided herself. It was an easy matter to push all those unpleasant memories aside. As long as she kept reminding herself that she wasn't the same person she'd been all those years ago she would manage just fine.

But, coming out of the adjoining bathroom after a refreshing shower, coming face to face with Sebastian, she wasn't so sure.

A mixture of shock and outrage, coupled with something she couldn't define, had her frozen, her hands above her head as she rough-dried her hair, her fingers turning to stone in the fluffy folds of the towel she was using. Then the sultry slide of his black eyes released her locked muscles and she whipped the towel down, covering her nakedness.

The gall of the man! The utter, utter gall! Oh, how dared he . . . ?

His eyes swept up to meet her own, and the look in the burning depths made hot colour sweep over every last inch of her skin. She hadn't blushed for years—not since she had taken charge of her own life—and the fact that this ogre had the power to do that to her made her very angry indeed. And her voice was harsh as she hurled at him, 'Get out of my room, damn you!'

'You were not always so unwelcoming, Charlotte.'

The velvet, sexily accented softness of his voice, the way he said her name, his despicable reminder of the way she had been, confused her emotions, jumbling them up until she didn't know whether she was on her head or her heels, and through that turmoil grew the need to retaliate, to hurt him as he had hurt her. And her voice was thin and acidic, and she clutched the towel against her until her knuckles gleamed whitely, telling him, 'I didn't welcome you. I just put up with you. There is a difference.'

'*Mentiras*!' The lithe, powerful body stiffened immediately, his jawline taut with cold aggression as he accused her of lying. He could accuse her, but he could never be sure. The thought was a triumph in itself. She was learning lessons from him and learning them fast. Before she lost the stimulus she manufactured a look of total uninterest and told him coolly, 'As it's all well in the past, the subject's academic, wouldn't you say?' She shrugged, taking care not to dislodge the towel by so much as a millimetre. 'Anyway, what was it you wanted?'

'Simply to tell you that Teresa will serve dinner in fifteen minutes.' His voice would have frozen a raging inferno, and the cold breath of his anger touched her, raising goose-bumps. Merely a reaction to the high she'd been on, she told herself, and nothing at all to do with the way he looked.

As if he would like to kill her but wouldn't demean himself by touching her.

For the first time she noted he was already dressed for dinner, in sleekly fitting black trousers, oyster silk shirt and a superbly cut, colour-toned lightweight dinner-jacket. He was, as ever, spectacular, the icy anger of his wounded Andalucían pride giving a diamond-hard brilliance to his brooding dark male beauty.

It wasn't outward appearances that counted, she reminded herself, looking quickly away from him, because the merest glimpse of him had always sent her senses haywire. It was what was on the inside that mattered, and inside Sebastian Machado was as rotten as a hundred-year-old egg!

'You've changed your habits,' she remarked, doing her best to sound offhand, not willing to let him know that being in the same room with him threw up the kind of emotions that were definitely bad for her health. 'Dinner was never served before ten, and it was more often nearer eleven before we sat down to eat. And I'm not very hungry, anyway.'

'Hungry or not, you will eat.' His black eyes glittered into the topaz defiance of hers. 'The meal was brought forward because you have been travelling for the best part of the day. You must be tired.'

'How thoughtful!' Charley made it sound like a sneer. 'Another change. Thoughtfulness was never one of your strong points, as I recall.' She would have stalked back into the bathroom, if she'd had the nerve. But she wasn't too sure about the security of the towel, and she wasn't at all sure that he wouldn't stalk right after her and drag her back. No one left the presence unless expressly commanded to do so.

But he merely reiterated, 'Fifteen minutes,' and walked out of the room as if he couldn't bear to be near her for one more moment. And that makes two of us! Charley fulminated, her face going white with temper as she snatched up the skirt and blouse she had put out earlier.

Fully dressed, she didn't look as if she were about to light any fires. But then that wasn't the object, was it? And if the features that stared back at her from the mirror were strained and pinched, could it be wondered at?

A heavier hand than normal with the make-up she'd brought with her didn't make her feel any better, but banished the wrung-out-old-dishcloth look. Got to keep my end up, she rallied herself as she left her room. And so far she was doing fine. If she was keeping score she would give six to one and half a dozen to the other!

Rooting around a bit, she discovered a lavishly arranged table in the smaller, more intimate of the three courtyards that bounded the graceful fortress of the house. In the centre, one of the fountains for which the house was named permeated the soft darkness with the song of water. The Moors, coming from dry lands, had deeply appreciated the gift of water; it refreshed the eyes and ears as much as it refreshed a parched throat. And here, as in many parts of the province, the Moorish influence was strong.

And the night was richly perfumed, an evocative mixture of roses, lilies, rosemary and oleander that went straight to her head, more intoxicating than wine. And added to the music of the water was the rustle of palms from the gardens beyond, and lamps in iron brackets cast a glimmering, magical light, enhancing

the quality of soft mystery—merely hinting, never revealing, giving a glimpse of the curving purity of a
white rose, heavy with fragrance, drawing a gauzy veil
over the half-seen line of a piece of marble statuary...

Charley caught her thoughts and slapped them
roughly down. Once, years ago, she would have nearly
gone out of her tiny mind at the thought of dining
alone with her idolised Sebastian in such a romantic
setting. She would happily have licked his boots in
adoring gratitude.

But not any more. And when he stepped out from
the arcaded shadows she put the wave of pain that
tore through her down to a mangled nervous system—
brought on, of course, by what he had made her do.
For some reprehensible reasons of his own—spawned
from that twisted, cruel mind of his—he had forced
her to stay here when all she had wanted was his
agreement to end formally a marriage that must be
as distasteful to him as it was to her.

'Only two place settings?' Charley ran light fingers
over the white damask cloth that covered the circular
table. 'Olivia not with you at the moment?' He had
already accepted that her physical appearance had
changed, and now she had to show him that her whole
attitude had changed. She was in control of her life
and her destiny, was a fully adult woman and not an
overgrown, sheltered child. So to begin with she could
show him that she could mention that woman's name
without having hysterics!

He paced towards her and pulled out a chair, an
eloquent black brow drifting upwards as he instructed softly, 'Sit. Olivia has not visited Cadiz, to
my knowledge, for a long time. Wine?'

She didn't believe him, but wasn't going to give him the satisfaction of arguing. In any case, it didn't matter. The wine he gave her was a wonderfully smooth twelve-year-old Rioja, and even before Sebastian had seated himself opposite, lighting the candle in the centre of the table and slotting the protective glass covering in place, Teresa was with them, a grinning Pilar bringing up the rear, both bearing huge covered dishes.

She was, Charley recognised, being given the works. There were three delicious salads to dip into: pimentos with anchovy, artichoke hearts with tuna, and a *Sevillana*—lovely crisp lettuce, sweet fresh tomatoes, tarragon, olives and hard-boiled egg. Then came the utterly delicious legacy of the Moors—spinach with almonds and raisins, spiced with cinnamon and nutmeg. And who would resist Teresa's sizzling hot giant prawns, cooked in chilli and garlic-flavoured olive oil? Charley couldn't, though she knew Greg would have frowned on such lavish excess.

The relaxing setting, the superb food and wine—not to mention Teresa's careful attendance—had helped her to unwind, to forget the vexed question of what she was doing here in the first place and remember that she'd been too uptight to eat any breakfast, or anything on the plane coming over, and only when Teresa and Pilar finally withdrew did she forget the sensual delights of the palate and come back to her senses with a bang.

Subdued, misty lamplight played across the table, on the ivory-toned fabric of Sebastian's jacket, on the lean, olive-toned fingers as they deftly stripped the peel from an orange, leaving his face shadowy and mysterious. And although she knew that the fruit was

far more juicily sweet and delicious than any that
could be bought back in England, Charley shook her
head and clamped her lips together as he offered her
a segment.

Greg would have forty fits if he could see her now.
And she wouldn't blame him. Everything, just everything, was a celebration of the senses: sight, sound,
taste and scent, a sybaritic pandering to all that was
sensual. It was a setting fit for high romance, certainly not a setting the down-to-earth Greg would have
been comfortable with.

But it was nothing but an illusion. Unconsciously,
Charley sighed, and Sebastian said harshly, 'Missing
your portly lover, Charlotte? Wishing he were here in
my place?'

'Naturally,' she came back at once, stiffening her
spine defensively. It wasn't the truth, though.

She missed Greg, of course she did, missed his
common-sense attitude and straightforward character.
But she couldn't wish him here. He didn't go a bundle
on illusions. He liked to know what he was getting.
A meal like this, in such a setting, would have made
him uneasy. He would have preferred a well lit room,
two courses of solid English fare—not this relaxed
dipping about all over the place—and a decent half-
pint of real ale to go with it. That she had—up until
now, of course—wholeheartedly enjoyed it all would
have annoyed him, because her enjoyment would not
have been something he could have shared.

'Are you in love with him?'

The question was posed with perfect seriousness,
but he leaned forward, into the pool of light, and the
sultry eyes were mocking. She met them warily, not
knowing how to answer. She had been 'in love' before,

and it had nearly driven her out of her mind. What she felt for Greg in no way resembled the extravagant, profligate passion that had made her a willing slave to this dark devil's merest glance.

He'd made her an addict, destroyed her self-respect, made her incapable of thinking of anything or anyone but him. So no, what she felt for Greg was nothing like that. And neither did she want it to be! Never again would any man enslave her to such a degrading extent.

But she wasn't about even to try to explain, to tell him that she had agreed to marry Greg because he would make a good father for the children they both wanted to have some day, because he was steady and sensible and he respected her, and allowed her to respect herself, and would never, ever try to overwhelm her. He wouldn't know how to begin. So she said baldly, 'None of your business. The only thing that need concern us is the ending of our marriage.' She finished the wine in her glass, congratulating herself on putting him in his place. And, just to let him know that he needn't think he'd got the upper hand just because she'd agreed to stay, she pronounced airily, 'I might decide to leave in the morning. I could always file for a legal separation.'

'Which would take twelve months, leaving you no better off than you are now—without my formal agreement to a divorce,' he pointed out drily. 'Besides, I wouldn't bother if I were you. You're no more in love with your accountant than I am.' He refilled her glass, right to the brim, and she knotted her brows at him.

'Clairvoyant, are you? How can you possibly know what I feel——?'

'I know far more than you give me credit for, *mi esposa.*' His voice had the cutting edge of steel. 'You may wonder what you are doing here, why I should allow you within miles of my home. Let me tell you...' Lean fingers beat softly against white damask. 'You once accused me of a deed so shameful that I vowed to have revenge, to make you, too, taste the kind of pain that turns the soul to iron. That is why I had you watched, had your every movement reported back to me.'

Silenced, Charley stared into the glowing darkness of his eyes, her mouth going dry. Revenge was a hateful word, walking down the years, biding its time, waiting for the right, the most devastating opportunity. Was that why she was here now, neatly trapped in this elegant, sumptuous web?

And she had walked right into it. But she wasn't afraid. Why should she be? He could do nothing to her except make her wait for another year before she could be completely rid of him.

Her eyes never wavering, she gave a tiny shrug and twisted the stem of her glass between her fingers. 'Bully-boy tactics don't suit you, Sebastian.' Then she took the fight right back to him. 'I accused you of two shameful deeds, or had you forgotten? Which one of the two made you throw your money away on the expense of having me watched? Killing your own brother, or carrying on your affair with Olivia after we were married?'

He ignored her taunts, merely watched her. His half-hooded eyes boring into hers as if he could reach right into her soul, his fingers stilled now, lamplight playing on those darkly beautiful features, making a shifting, unreadable mask of them, a mask she suddenly ached to tear away with frenzied fingers.

She was beginning to shake inside. He alone could make her do that. But she wasn't going to let him have that effect on her. She wouldn't tolerate it. She lifted her glass to her lips and swallowed, and reminded him coldly, 'If you recall, you didn't refute either accusation. Because you couldn't?' If, at the time, he had even attempted to, she would have been only too happy to listen, pathetically eager to believe whatever he said, even then, even after Olivia had told her the truth. She had been bewitched by him.

But he had said nothing, not a single word to defend himself against either accusation.

'Did I need to?' Inflexible Gaditano pride spiked every syllable, and his eyes were coldly expressionless as he leaned back into the shadows. 'I think the fact that you came here in person, instead of putting your request through a solicitor, speaks for itself.' His velvet voice dropped, softening hypnotically, sending shivers down her spine. 'Had you really believed me capable of the shameful deed of murder, you would not have come near me—let alone agreed to stay with me. That tells me you didn't believe, even then.' White teeth gleamed suddenly against the shadowy darkness of his face. 'Therefore, what really sent you scurrying away, back to England, where you mistakenly thought you could forget me, was the belief that I went to Olivia's bed. You were too much of a child then to cope with that kind of jealousy, to think it through.'

He stood up, pushing back his chair, looking pagan in the drifting, shadowy lamplight. 'You are a child no longer; the appeal is still there, but enhanced by excitement. You have become an opponent worthy of my steel. Is that not so?'

He came nearer and she stood up quickly, willing the shakiness out of her legs, managing a commendably wobble-free voice as she pushed her chin in the air and argued, 'We have nothing to fight about, not any more,' absolutely unprepared for his softly spoken,

'Surely you see the battle that emerges? But don't be afraid—it will reach a successful conclusion.' A lean hand cupped her elbow as he escorted her inside. 'May I suggest that you give some thought to what I have said? It would ensure that victory comes more quickly. I grow impatient, *querida*. I have waited too long. However . . .' His shrug was almost too graceful to be borne. 'Some women, like some wines, take longer than others to mature. It is a process that can't be hurried, yet the results are worth waiting for.'

CHAPTER THREE

IN THE past, Charley had never tired of looking out over the deep water harbour with its crane-spiked waterfront teeming with tugs, ferries, merchant ships and cruise liners, but this morning she really wasn't seeing anything.

Like a coward, she had crept out of the house very early and had wandered her way through the web of narrow streets until thirst had driven her into a bar for coffee, and after that she'd found herself at the harbour without even consciously aiming her feet in that direction.

And now the sun was burning the mist from the water and the inside of her head felt as if it were full of unravelled knitting, because she'd spent a wakeful, restless night doing her best to avoid thinking over what Sebastian had said.

In his typical lordly fashion he had instructed her to think over what he had said concerning her reasons for leaving him in the first place, her own supposed lack of belief in the most damning of the two accusations she'd hurled at him.

Well, she wasn't going to! The time for soul-searching was long gone. Her marriage to Sebastian was over in all but name, and a contented future with Greg lay just around the corner. And that was the way she wanted it. Yes, most certainly, that was the way she wanted it!

Aware that she was squinting against the rapidly increasing glare of the sun, she fished her dark glasses out of her bag and slid them on to her nose. And from right behind her Sebastian said, 'What a surprise,' his tone very dry.

Charley froze. And, without turning, she asked crossly, 'What are you doing here?'

Did he have his spies out, even here? Or had he followed her himself, a silent, watchful shadow, dogging her footsteps? Like Nemesis. But the dryness increased until his voice was utterly withering as he reminded her, 'I had business at the harbour. I visit frequently. Don't tell me you'd forgotten.'

'Totally,' she lied contentiously, and turned to face him, feeling, quite insanely, much more relaxed. She had never so much as bent the truth in the past, never argued, had always been anxious to please, slavishly devoted. Giving as good as she got was fun, she decided, her sparkling amber eyes hidden behind dark glasses.

Of course she remembered his frequent visits to the offices at the commercial docks, the times she had walked this way on the off-chance of seeing him, wondering if he would be in this area or in the Machado office block on the outskirts of the city. He had rarely spoken about his work, probably seeing her as too flea-brained to be interested in the export empire that had been started by his grandfather.

But whenever Olivia had come out to Cadiz he'd spent long hours with her, discussing business—or so he had said.

'Then I can only conclude that the dreariness of the British weather and the added boredom of your job has damaged your brain.'

He was grinning at her, calling her bluff, his black eyes sharp and knowing, and she countered with as much enthusiasm as she could manage, 'Far from it. I love my job; it's much more stimulating than trying to be the dutiful wife of a wealthy Spaniard! All that sitting around with nothing to do but attend to the flowers, speaking when I was spoken to, wondering what time you'd be home. If at all. So stimulating, in fact, that unimportant things like whether you visit the harbour or not got pushed right out of my head.'

'Is that so? Maybe I should have asked Ignacia to teach you how to scrub floors.'

The sultry look was back in his eyes. It did things to her. And she couldn't bear it!

She looked away quickly, watching the *vapor* from Puerto appear through the last few remaining wisps of mist that hung over the bay as she willed the too rapid beats of her heart to slow down to normal. Hitching the narrow leather strap of her bag higher on her shoulder, she said coolly, 'Shouldn't you be at work or something? Don't let me detain you.' She had never been able to detain him before; he had spent the majority of his time chained to his desk. Except when Olivia had been around, of course.

But she wasn't going to remind him of that. She would never mention that woman's name to him again. And Sebastian denied smoothly, 'I have taken a holiday.'

As far as she knew today wasn't a public holiday, with carnival or fiesta an excuse for everything to shut down. But he definitely wasn't dressed for the office. She couldn't see him sitting behind his huge desk wearing that sleeveless black body-hugging T-shirt and those casual white lightweight trousers.

'How nice. Do enjoy your day, won't you?' Charley swept off along the Avenida del Puerto, braving the thunderous traffic, her brisk stride echoing, she hoped, the tart finality of her words. No way was she prepared to spend the day with him, or even a part of it. She had made up her mind that the best way to deal with the coming four weeks was to keep well out of his way, to think of him and of the past as little as possible.

'I have taken far more than one day.' His voice was as smooth as honeyed cream, and Charley flinched as his big hand shot out to drag her away from the rapidly approaching wheels of a great snarling truck. 'Four weeks, to be exact.'

'Hell!' Charley closed her eyes as she leant weakly back against him, her body melding into his as if it belonged. If he was going to hound her for the whole of that time she would probably go mad!

His naked arm slid around her tiny waist, his fingers splayed warmly across her ribcage. She wondered distractedly if he could feel the frantic hammer beats of her heart and knew that he must have done, but had misinterpreted the cause of the fluster, when he said silkily, 'Allow me to guide you. I would hate to think my presence had driven you to prefer suicide under wheels of a juggernaut.'

Sarcastic lump of hatefulness! Charley fumed as he expertly dodged the wild flow of traffic and finally deposited her neatly on the edge of the Plaza Sevilla.

'Coffee?' he asked, one brow lifting urbanely. 'Or perhaps you need something stronger.'

'Let's stop fooling around,' Charley snapped out, small hands flapping at him, brushing him away. Enough was enough. 'I don't need you to see me over the road. I don't need you to buy coffee or tag along. In short——' big amber eyes glared behind sheltering dark lenses, the line of her mouth very determined '—I don't need you at all.'

'Oh, but you do,' he contradicted, his teeth white against the tanned olive tones of his skin. 'You need my agreement to the divorce you're so suddenly anxious to get.' He smiled, but there was no humour in it. Just naked aggression.

Charley scowled right back at him. As she had decided moments earlier, enough was enough, and she conceded honestly, her hands slicing sideways impatiently, 'I stand corrected. I do need you for that. But I can't understand why you should insist I stay here. And neither,' she tacked on tartly, 'does Greg.'

If she had hoped that by bringing her next husband into the discussion she could get him to admit that his bargaining position was as ridiculous as it was pointless she was disappointed, because all he said was, 'Good. At last you are willing to talk. Perhaps even to think things through. Come, let us walk.'

She had no clear idea of where they were going and only the haziest notion of why she was still at his side as they slipped from one narrow street to another. The only thing she knew for sure was that to do as he said in this respect was easier than picking a fight. He was quite capable of forcing her to go with him.

But even he wasn't capable of forcing her to 'think things through'—as he kept suggesting. He might be able to control her physical movements for the next month, but he couldn't control what was going on inside her head. And why should she dredge up the past, with all its grief and pain? It was over, and thinking of what had happened, and why it had happened, would be pointless.

Only when they emerged into the brilliant sunlight did she stop grumbling away inside her head. They had come to the Campo del Sur, the broad walkway on the city's southern limits, the blue waters of the Atlantic washing against white stones and, looming above them, the awesome Baroque block of the cathedral, its golden dome glittering in the white light reflected from the whitewashed buildings.

The painful tug of loss hurt her heart. Sebastian had introduced her to this fascinating city, and she hadn't been able to help falling in love with it. And then he had driven her from it. Just one more thing to make her hate him!

But she didn't hate him, she reminded herself. He was nothing to her, not even an enemy now.

Thankfully he seemed as disinclined to talk as she, but her mouth turned down at the corners as she noted the frankly admiring glances he earned from every passing female. Every last one of them would run a mile if they knew what he was really like, but the silly fools couldn't see beyond the superb physique, the brooding, beautiful face.

Yet who was she to be so scornful? Hadn't she been dazzled by all that potent masculinity five years ago, whirled out of the reach of any sane thought, made totally oblivious to her aunt's tart warnings, by the blinding quality of his charm?

'I'm sure you must be hungry. I know I am.'

Charley glanced up sharply, his voice, cutting into the quiet self-condemnation of her thoughts, startling her. He sounded too friendly to be true, given all the circumstances. But she wasn't going to question the warmth of his tone. Delving into his motives didn't pay, not unless you were prepared to face something dark and devious and definitely unpleasant. And she wasn't.

She nodded vaguely. 'A little.' And looked quickly away, fixing her eyes on the hazy distance of the blue horizon. She didn't want to look at him.

But when he'd seated her at a shaded table on the pavement outside a café he leaned over and tweaked the dark glasses off her neat nose, and she gasped a protest. Did he always know what was going on in her mind? Was that why he was forcing her to look at him, see him properly—because he had known she hadn't wanted to?

'We are in the shade, so you don't need them.' His deep, sexy voice made her grit her teeth. 'Besides, your eyes are as beautiful as ever they were. I want to see them.'

The compliment, facile as it was, unnerved her. It was unfair. But then, when had he ever been fair?

'I can't imagine why,' she snapped, rallying, forcing a brittle smile for the waiter who had brought out the half-bottle of chilled Manzanilla and the lemon Sebastian had ordered to go with the *papelon surtido*—the mixed fried fish—he had bought from the nearby *freiduría*.

'You surprise me.' He sliced the lemon into wedges and squeezed the juice over the delicious-looking morsels. 'Four years ago your imagination was almost too fertile to be believed,' he told her with a cool glance of perception that brought angry colour to wash over her face.

'I didn't imagine the things Olivia told me,' she ground out, unable to help herself. 'I don't have that kind of mind!'

'Perhaps not,' he conceded smoothly, pouring wine. Charley watched the pale liquid in the elegantly curved glass, noted how quickly the condensation formed on the outside, and wondered if she had the energy to get up and walk away. 'But your imagination was keen enough to allow you to believe it. Or some of it, at least. It helped you to embellish what you'd been told until, like a child, you imagined things that weren't there—all those nameless horrors hiding in dark corners.' He shook his dark head, one lock of silky black hair falling to brush his arched brows. Charley didn't know whether the look of bitter reproof was manufactured or not, and wondered why she should care.

'There's no point in raking over the past—whether or not I let my imagination run away with me. Our marriage is over. It ended four years ago,' she pointed out, appalled by the wobble in her voice, afraid to look at him, because when his eyes probed hers they saw too much. They always had done. All those years ago he'd only had to look into her eyes to know that she'd fallen deeply and helplessly in love with him. Had that slavish look of adoration given him the idea of using her? Had it? Had she been almost as much to blame as he? There couldn't have been a more willing victim in the whole of history!

Unconsciously, she shook her head, setting the silky-soft strands of her short dark brown hair flying around her face, and Sebastian said with chilling ferocity, 'Don't think that because you walked out on me I considered the marriage over. Nothing changed because you were a foolish child with an over-active imagination.'

'You amaze me,' she countered, her chin jutting. 'Four years and not a word. How long would it have taken you—another forty? You considered our marriage far from over and yet you did nothing. Not a damn thing!' Except have her watched, set his spies on her. The golden scorn in her eyes changed to dark wariness, and he smiled, surprising her yet again.

'It's too hot to fight. In any event, my intention is not to argue with you, merely to help you to see things clearly.'

She didn't want to—— Quickly, she chopped off that particular train of thought. He was right, it was too hot to snap and snarl at each other. Also pointless. And at least here, beneath the shade of the colourful scarlet and yellow awning, enjoying the welcome breeze from the water, it was cooler. And it could have been restful if it weren't for his ability to make her so stingingly aware of him all the time.

But it wasn't anything sexual, not now, she told herself as she took a strengthening sip of the deliciously crisp wine. It was because they were at loggerheads over the divorce, because he had put such an untenable condition on his agreement. That was all. And, that being so, she must accept it for what it was and stop getting so wound up.

'So tell me about your work in England.' His tanned, muscular forearms were resting on the tabletop. The glistening skin was slightly roughened by fine dark hairs. Charley felt her throat close up and took another drink. Her hand was shaking.

'It might bore you,' she stalled, not liking the sudden thought that her duties were rather repetitive.

Helping Dev run the hotel-cum-conference centre, with a few forays into the leisure activities side of it, would sound pretty tame by comparison with a trading empire that sent merchantmen ranging over the oceans of the world with the wealth of Spain, with fruit and wine, almonds and olives, leather from Ubrique, carpets from Arcos de la Frontera and colourful capes and ponchos from Grazalema—the list was endless and far more romantic than routine linen checks with the chief housekeeper and suchlike!

'Then tell me something that will not bore me. Here, try this.' He popped a morsel of crisply fried fish into her mouth. 'Tell me how you came to meet the fat man you think you want to marry.'

Charley choked on the battered prawn, and as soon as she got her breath back she told him haughtily, 'Greg is not fat. I don't know how you got that idea into your head.'

'I have seen pictures. I am not blind.' He popped another morsel between her parted lips, his dark head tilted sideways, those sultry eyes drifting across her features, coming to rest on her mouth. 'I simply find it incredible that you should even consider replacing me with him.'

In spite of herself Charley's lips twitched and the acid comment she'd been about to make on the subject of spying flew out of her head. That natural arrogance was almost unbelievable. His big opinion of himself—which would have made her despise any other man—merely amused her, made her feel almost tender.

Sternly resisting the impulse to brush that wayward lock of black hair back off his forehead, she decided that to tell him that outward appearances meant nothing, that what lay beneath the surface was all that mattered, would diminish her.

Their marriage was over, whether Sebastian chose to recognise it or not, and once the divorce came through she would marry Greg. So she would be adult about it—one of them had to be—and answer his question in a civilised manner.

'There's an eighteen-hole golf course attached to the complex where I work. Greg's been a member since it opened, but until his mother died, about a year ago, he didn't socialise—relax after the game in the bar, or attend any of the golf club functions.'

'And after his mother died he took to drink.' Sebastian refilled her glass, and the sympathetic shake of his head was completely spurious, she knew it was. But she didn't rise.

'Hardly.' Greg could make half a pint of ale last all evening. 'But he did begin to attend the odd function. And that was how we met, since you said you wanted to know. I was there on one particular evening, standing in for one of the bar staff who'd failed to turn up. We got talking.'

And although Greg hadn't said as much, not that first time, he'd been lonely. He'd been divorced some time ago and his mother had recently died and the house had been empty. And she had sympathised, because she'd known what loneliness was.

Her unsociable working hours had meant that she hadn't had the opportunity to make friends outside the other members of staff. And they had mostly had their own families. So when Greg had asked if they could meet on her next day off, maybe go for a walk and find a quiet pub where they served decent food, she had agreed. She'd been tired of spending her time off back in her room, tucked away at the top of the hotel, washing her hair and her smalls, or catching the bus into town to watch a film she hadn't really wanted to see.

'And he asked you to go out with him?' Sebastian surmised. 'How nice. Did you tell him you were married? Probably not. What did you do? Did he make love to you?'

'Of course not!' Charley shot back. Was he implying that she was the kind of woman who would allow a man to make love to her on a first date? He was beginning to infuriate her. She mustn't let that happen. She had to stay calm and rational.

'It rained,' she said.

From his expression, her apparent *non sequitur* amused him inordinately. She ignored him and concentrated on what was left of the food.

And yes, in the event it had rained. Walking had been out of the question and she had ended up back at his home, cooking their meal. And in the evening he had lit the fire, and they'd sat in front of it, cradling mugs of tea in their hands and talking. And it had been nice to be in a real home again, the curtains closed against the unfriendly weather, a fire in the hearth, someone to talk to, someone who was interested in her and her opinions.

And gradually, over the following weeks and months, they had got to know each other well, to like and respect each other. Their dates had settled into an easy routine. They hadn't needed to throw money away on entertainment; they were perfectly capable of making their own. And somehow Charley had found herself in possession of the key to his home. If her day off came on a weekday, Greg had told her, she could let herself in, make use of the place, and be waiting for him when he came home from work. It was better than aimlessly wandering round the shops or being cooped up in her room back at the hotel.

So it had seemed natural that, on the days she spent there, she should tidy up, put the contents of the linen basket into the washing-machine, have a hot meal waiting when he came home. The cosy domesticity was something she had missed. It reminded her of the time when her parents had been alive and living in England, before everything had gone so terribly wrong. And it helped her to push the year of her marriage even further into the recesses of her mind. At the Casa de las Surtidores there had been servants to do everything. She hadn't needed to lift a finger. No one had needed her.

Now Greg needed her, and that gave her a nice comfortable feeling . . .

'Such a silence.' Sebastian's voice was drily sardonic. 'Am I to take it that there is nothing more to say on the subject of your passionate courtship? I'm only amazed you didn't expire from over-excitement.'

Her fingers tightened round her fork, the knuckles gleaming whitely beneath the fine skin. But her voice was frigidly controlled as she told him, 'It didn't always rain, I assure you,' and allowed him to make what he liked of that.

His eyes turned thunderous. A muscle jerked with sudden menace at the side of his hard jaw. Whatever he'd made of her remark, he obviously didn't like it. Tough. He'd been needling her, sending her to the brink of fury, so what did she care if he didn't like being pricked in return?

'In my experience, it is always raining in that country of yours,' he bit back at her, the tips of his fingers beating a slow tattoo on the top of the table. 'Nothing good ever happened to me there.'

'Really?' Her voice was stiff with the effort of containing all that pent-up passion she had never expected or wanted to experience again. 'You spent enough time there to meet Olivia and begin your affair.' Her face burned with dull colour. Damn! She had vowed not to mention that woman's name to him ever again, and yet here she was, sounding like a jealous wife! He'd think he still had the power to hurt her. She would have to correct that impression before it took root in his devious brain. Feeling her temper rise to blistering proportions, she lashed out. 'And if that wasn't "good" enough for you, you inherited the family business while you were in my country. Your brother conveniently died there, didn't he? And everything fell into your lap.'

Even before the last syllable had snapped past her lips she knew she had gone too far, and regretted it. Her fingers shaking, she gathered her handbag and stood up. Being anywhere near him was a dreadful mistake. He brought out the worst in her.

She moved away, leaving him at the table, then paused. She felt awkward now, ashamed of herself for allowing him to needle her into retaliating so harshly. Turning, a tentative apology hovering on her lips, she shuddered, going suddenly cold.

The fallen-angel face had turned satanic in its dark and unforgiving pride.

Charley dragged in a deep breath and fled.

CHAPTER FOUR

CHARLEY leant her arms on the cool stone sill of one of the windows in her room. The night air was still and warm, whispering softly against the upper part of her body through the almost transparent cotton of her sleeveless nightgown.

Below her the garden was a moon-silvered mystery, a place of softly rustling enchantment, of sleepy seductive fragrances, stroked and caressed by the ever present watery music of the fountains. She sighed, her eyes troubled, knowing her unease was not entirely due to the way she had avoided Sebastian, hiding in the maze of bustling narrow streets, returning at twilight to tell Teresa she would eat from a tray in her room tonight.

She owed Sebastian an apology for the snide things she had said at the end of lunch today, and she should have faced up to him and delivered it at dinner this evening. But the fact that she had avoided him in such a cowardly fashion wasn't the end of the world. She could apologise in the morning. No, her melancholia was more deep-seated than that. It was this place, she recognised, the loveliness of it, the memories it evoked.

When Sebastian had first brought her here as his bride she had been overwhelmed. In many ways she had been childlike, out of her depth in surroundings of such beauty and opulence. Nothing he had told her during their brief and, for her at least, wildly emotional courtship had prepared her for this.

Kicking with resistance at first, then with a sudden, fluid ease that shocked her, her mind flew back to the first time they met. The circumstances could hardly have been more fraught.

Three days earlier Charley had heard that both her parents had been killed, their car going off the road in a violent thunderstorm during their motoring holiday among the isolated white villages scattered on the southern slopes of the Sierra Nevada. They had left the midsummer heat of the coast to find the cooler air of the mountains and had found, instead, oblivion.

She and Freda had flown out to Rota, too stunned to do more than function like automatons.

The funeral had been very quiet. Charley had barely registered the presence of the tall stranger who had accompanied her parents' Spanish solicitor, Señor Avila, until, back at the modern bungalow just above the wide, sweeping beaches of Rota, on the northern-most tip of the Bay of Cádiz, he had introduced himself as Sebastian Machado. Her father, he had told her, had been known to him. Not only had they met socially, but the older man had invested in his company, buying a small block of shares. Shares which would now belong to Charley.

He had been kind and sympathetic and supportive, qualities the grieving Charley—or Charlotte, as Sebastian had insisted on calling her—had been greatly in need of at the time. And the fact that he had been as fluent in English as he was in his own language had endeared him to Freda to begin with.

'Such a blessing when it comes to helping us get through the tangle of red tape,' that lady had stated.

'Señor Avila means well, I know, but his English is pidgin at best, and the only Spanish word I know is *gracias*!'

But later, during the few days Freda had to spare from her business back in England, Charley had sensed a change in her attitude towards the impossibly attractive Spaniard. She had become brusque, almost surly, her eyes looking at him with suspicion.

Sebastian had appeared every day as they carried on with the sad task of sorting through the contents of the bungalow. He seemed to be drawn like a magnet. Just as she had been. She hadn't been able to take her eyes off him, and although she seemed to be tongue-tied when he was around she was sure he only had to look at her to know how crazy she was about him. She had never met anyone like him before.

On the third evening after the funeral Sebastian had taken them both out to dinner, choosing one of the cosmopolitan restaurants that had come into being because of the proximity of the large American naval base. Freda hadn't wanted to accept the invitation, saying it wasn't right, not so soon . . .

But Sebastian had insisted, as only a man possessing such oceans of unforced charm could do, and Charley—all a-flutter—had rushed out to buy something suitable to wear. Black, of course, but daringly off-the-shoulder, and when her aunt had seen her, all dressed up, with her mousy hair left loose for a change and falling almost to her waist, her smear of pink lipstick and her incongruous dress, she had remarked snappily, 'I dread to think what your mother would say if she could see you now!'

And Charley's eyes had flooded with tears and her mouth had still been trembling when Sebastian had arrived. He had offered her his hand, as if knowing how near her heart was to breaking, and she had taken it, clinging as if to a lifeline. It was the first time they had touched each other, and the effect, for her, was earth-shattering.

He alone seemed to know how she felt; he alone seemed to really care. Señor Avila had been kind, of course, but he was a busy man with little time for anything other than the business in hand. And Freda was—well, Freda. Sensible, brusque and unsentimental. And she had said, over dinner that night, 'We have to leave the day after tomorrow; I do have a business to run. And as you've been so kind, Señor Machado, might I impose further on your good nature and ask if you would ask the solicitor on our behalf if he could arrange for someone reliable to remove the clothing and bedlinen—things like that—and donate them to some charity? The furniture and other effects will stay *in situ* until after probate, naturally. And of course, whoever you find must give the place a thorough cleaning before the keys are returned to Señor Avila.'

Charley's heart had thumped alarmingly. She thought it might burst with panic and misery. She had counted on staying longer. There were things belonging to her parents she would like to keep: a beautiful ecru silk blouse her mother had kept for special occasions, her father's fishing hat—it had been a family joke for as long as she could remember. She didn't want all their things to be bundled away as her aunt suggested. It would be like saying her parents had never existed.

And Sebastian had said, with the first touch of steel she had heard in his beautiful voice, 'I understand you have business commitments you can't neglect. But if Charlotte would like to stay on for a while I will make myself responsible for her well-being. If she spends a little more time here in the area her parents chose for their retirement, she may more easily come to terms with her loss.'

So of course, that clinched it. It gave Charley the courage to defy her aunt for the first time since she'd lived with her. And it was the long summer holiday, she wouldn't be returning to college until late September, and there would be nothing to do back in Harrow except grieve for her parents and regret the haste with which their retirement home had been cleared out and locked up.

And there had been the other thing, she admitted honestly, her cheeks going pink as she had prepared to go against her aunt's wishes. She had fallen head over heels in love with Sebastian. She couldn't look at him without feeling giddy. She couldn't bear the thought of never seeing him again.

So she had stayed on and had listened with only half of one ear as Freda, on departing, had warned, 'You're nineteen years old and I can't force you to come back to England. But you're as wet behind the ears as the day you were born. And I don't trust that man. He probably wants to get you into his bed, but that's only part of it. I don't know what he's up to. But, for your own good, don't sign anything until you've had it independently translated, and don't let him make love to you. It might be quite an experience, but you wouldn't be able to handle it.'

Six weeks later they were married in a quiet civil ceremony. She hadn't invited her aunt. Sebastian had told her he had fallen in love with her, almost on sight, and she had believed him. Then.

And on the day they had married she knew no more about him than the very little he had told her. Both his parents were dead. His mother had died when he was two years old, his father when he was twenty. He'd had an older brother, Fernando, but he had died tragically a few years ago. He was now alone, had no family apart from a handful of distant cousins. He lived in Cadiz, and his work was something to do with the docks and shipping.

Nothing he had told her had prepared her for this, for the opulence of his lifestyle, the size and prestige of his business empire. All those hazy, half-formed dreams of settling down with him, keeping a small whitewashed house clean and welcoming, preparing his meals, bearing his children, had been abruptly shattered.

Charley stirred uneasily, dragging in her breath as pain lanced through her. Nothing had prepared her for his lovemaking, either.

During their whirlwind courtship she had received nothing more than the touch of his hand on hers, the chastest of kisses. Vaguely, her body had told her that there should be more, but he had always been circumspect, putting her aside with a soft word when her body, of its own accord, had demanded more.

She had never had a lover; she'd been too sheltered—and not very interested, either. Certainly, during her year at college, she'd made friends with girls she'd instinctively known her parents wouldn't have approved of. The way they'd talked of their boyfriends would have made their hair fall out! But they had been safely in Spain, enjoying retirement. And, in any case, some of the clinical descriptions turned her stomach. And none of the male students had ever wanted to date her. She'd been too quiet, too studious and shy to interest them.

So when Sebastian had come to her room on their wedding night she'd had no idea what to expect—or only the barest details garnered from sex education in school and the raunchy, embarrassing confidences of her college friends.

The depth and breadth of his passion had over-whelmed her, making her nothing more than a quiv-ering, inarticulate mass of shattering sensation. Nothing had prepared her for this physical rapture. Nothing. She could hardly believe it was happening to her. And although she could never put into words how he made her feel, and although she was afraid that her clumsy inexperience must disappoint him, she ached for him on the nights when he didn't come to her, blaming herself.

And the more she had blamed herself and her gauche inexperience, the more woodenly anxious she had been when he had elected to share her bed. And, of, course, by that time Olivia had put in her first appearance since their marriage. And Olivia had been all that she, patently, was not: beautiful, assured, charming, her eyes flirting with Sebastian's when hers, Charley's, could only cling with anxious adoration.

But she had tried to cope, of course she had, tried not to mind that when Olivia made one of her many flying visits from the branch office in Plymouth her husband spent far more time with his employee than he did with his wife, ostensibly discussing business.

She had tried to improve her dress sense and to make a useful contribution to the running of his home.

But she had stopped trying when Olivia had told her the truth about her relationship with Sebastian, the affair that had begun all those years ago in England, the affair that would end in marriage when Charley had done her duty and given him an heir and could be thankfully put aside.

But it was all over now. Charley blinked, dragging herself back into the present. She had been so inexperienced when she had met him, deeply traumatised by the sudden death of both parents. She couldn't have been more vulnerable, and he had taken advantage. She'd been a push-over. But not any more.

So why did her heart twist inside her when a persuasive, velvet-soft voice from the garden below suggested, 'Come down. Walk with me; talk with me. The night is beautiful.'

'No.' Quickly she turned away from the window, her stomach tying itself in knots. Did he think she was mad? Did he think she would willingly expose herself to the danger of the moonlight, the scented garden and a veritable devil of a man?

But where was the danger? a tart inner voice demanded scornfully. If she was so all-fired adult, so cool and in control, why should she fear anything he could dish out?

Crossly, she slapped the voice down and climbed into bed, burrowing her head under the pillows. And surely she couldn't really hear that soft male laughter from the garden below—not under all this smothering lightness of feather and silk?

'Sleep well?' the sexy voice enquired as Charley came through the mist-shrouded gardens to find breakfast laid in a small panelled dining-room.

'Very.' It was a lie, of course. She'd barely closed her eyes through the long eternity of the night. But she wasn't telling him that. She sat at the table, her denim cut-offs topped by a soft green T-shirt at odds with the dignity of the room.

Taking care not to look directly at him, she straightened her shoulders and said stiffly, 'I'm sorry about yesterday. I had no right to imply that Fernando's death was good news.'

And she knew, with a clarity that made her want to weep, that it was the truth. She had never believed him capable of murder, of sneakily killing his own brother for financial gain. He had far too much pride and self-esteem. Even when the facts as read in the back copies of the English newspapers had corroborated the things Olivia had said, she hadn't believed, not in her heart. She had used the accusation of murder, and pretended—even to herself—that she believed it to excuse the way she had ended their marriage.

'Apology accepted.' He sounded more amused than anything, almost smug, as if he had known her acknowledgement of his innocence would inevitably come.

And Charley still couldn't meet his eyes, kept her own fixed on the glass of fresh orange juice he poured out for her. Because, despite his relaxed acceptance of her apology and the truth it underlined, there was a dreadful tension between them. It was making the hairs on the back of her neck stand on end, and heaven only knew what he would see in her eyes!

'I'm glad to see you have some sense!' Teresa swept into the room with a tray of steaming coffee and lightly toasted rolls. 'No more trays in your room, *señora*. Unless I have a signed statement from the doctor saying you lie at death's door!'

And the tension was broken, Charley smothering laughter as she at last met Sebastian's eyes. The intimacy of shared memories smouldered in the sultry depths, and his smile was a direct assault on her senses. Blood roared in her ears, her heart thumping as her own smile faded, leaving her lips trembling. She felt as if she were drowning.

But Sebastian dragged her from the strange morass, his idly amused, 'She gets worse. But what would the household do without her?' helping her to get her feet back on firmer ground.

She pulled in a deep, slow breath and poured coffee, watching him butter a roll and select a wafer-thin slice of Jabugo ham to go with it. Back to normal now, she didn't feel even the faintest stirrings of panic when he decided, 'We'll go to the beach this morning and swim before it gets too crowded. La Caleta, I think.'

'Why not?' she agreed, dribbling her preferred olive oil over a hot roll, her hands perfectly steady. She could hardly spend the entire four weeks trying to avoid him, strenuously objecting to whatever he suggested.

Besides, a swim would be refreshing, and although it was early in the season—only May—there would be other people on the beach; it wasn't as if there were any danger of the two of them being alone together in the little bay.

But, an hour later, Charley's senses went on to red alert. True, they weren't alone—there were several young Spanish mothers with their children playing in the soft yellow sand—but that didn't prevent the danger of the pointedly sensuous glide of those sultry black eyes as she peeled off the cut-offs and T-shirt to reveal the sleek one-piece swimsuit she had put on back at the house.

And her own eyes were riveted to the lean, tanned fingers as they unbuckled the belt at the waistband of his hip-hugging jeans. He had already discarded his loose-fitting black cotton shirt, and the sight of the oiled satin skin covering those hard wide shoulders, the dusting of fine black hair around the flat male nipples, sent an explosion of sheet-lightning sensation right down to the tips of her toes.

Alarmed, she forced her fascinated gaze away and turned, folding her clothes and putting them beside the canvas tote bag he had brought along, trying not to show how breathless she had suddenly become.

'See you,' she said, not looking at him, and forced herself to maintain a steady pace as she walked towards the water. It wouldn't do to let him see how he could still affect her. How it would amuse him; how he would gloat!

Steadily she waded into the water, cursing herself. Her mind might be cool and in control, but her wretched body was something else. And she wished, with quiet desperation, that Greg were here. Greg was safe and comfortable; he didn't set her body afire with the slightest glance—and who needed that? She didn't! Greg made her feel secure and respected and in control of her emotions. And that was what she needed!

The sun had burned through the morning mist, and the greeny-blue Atlantic swell reflected the bright rays like the facets of some giant gemstone. Charley took a deep breath and immersed herself, revelling in the cool, silky slide of the water as it lapped her skin.

She could stay out here for hours, she told herself, striking out with strong, unhurried strokes. She certainly wasn't going to lie around on the beach. He'd probably insist on smothering her with sunblock, and she wasn't falling for that old chestnut!

In any case, the danger she was seeing was probably all in her imagination. He couldn't possibly be trying to make her go weak at the knees. It was a knack he had. Nine times out of ten he wouldn't be aware that he was doing it!

No, it was just her reaction, that was all. A reaction she shared with every other woman who happened to be on the receiving end of one of those long, smouldering looks. There was no reason on earth for him to try and flirt with her. He had never truly wanted her, and he certainly hadn't loved her, and after a separation of four years' standing he could have no interest in her whatsoever.

And as for the way her body had burned up beneath the sultry black eyes that had wandered at will over its slender curves, well, that had to be down to last night's excursion into the past. A dangerous exercise, and one she had never previously allowed herself.

She could see herself now, see the way she had closed the bound copies of the old newspapers Olivia had dared her to consult. The way she had walked out on to the street, hailing a taxi to take her back to her aunt's flat in Harrow. She hadn't shed a tear, simply picked up the phone and dialled through to his Cadiz office. 'I'm home, in England, if you're interested. I won't be coming back. I can't live with a man who murdered his own brother—even if he did get away with it through lack of evidence.' She had heard the sharp drag of his indrawn breath and could imagine the blistering rage in his eyes. But he had said nothing to refute her accusation. Nothing at all. And when she could no longer stand the black silence she had snapped out, 'Olivia told me all about it, and your ongoing affair, and as far as I'm concerned she's more than welcome to you!' and banged down the receiver. And had vowed never to think of the past again.

Yet here she was, doing it again! Furious with herself, Charley made her mind go blank and turned on her back, floating, feeling the sun burning her face, gradually letting Greg creep into her mind, hoping he could fill it to the exclusion of all else.

But the hands that suddenly grasped her tiny waist, pulling her upright in the water, weren't Greg's hands. And Greg's eyes didn't look that wicked—they wouldn't know how.

Sea-water was streaming from his hair and shoulders, a myriad drops that glistened in the sunlight, making him look like some pagan sea-god.

Desperately, her feet fumbled for the bottom and failed to find it. She was out of her depth in more ways than one, she thought, near to panic. But he was supporting her, effortlessly treading water, his hard hands dragging her hips against the arch of his pelvis. Fear of what she knew he could do to her made her voice sharp.

'Don't do that! Sneaking up on me that way! You nearly gave me a heart attack!'

His blinding, charismatic grin was unforgivable. It stopped her in her tracks, the fists that had been lifted to beat him off treacherously uncurling, lying flat and suppliant against the wet, warm skin of his superb chest. She could feel his heart beating, and her own

went into overdrive as a big, slow wave crested,
thrusting her against him, and he taunted, 'So let me
see if it's still beating,' and slid both hands upwards,
curving them over her breasts.

'Like a crazy thing,' he confirmed, his black eyes
wicked, his long legs entwined with hers beneath the
water.

Charley made a strangled sound in her throat, desperately fighting the insistent need to melt against him,
to let him do what he would, struggling against the
almost overpowering urge to slide her hands down his
glorious body, slip his very brief briefs from their
anchorage on the bony projection of his hips, and
cradle his rampant manhood against the willing
softness of her belly.

It was crazy and it shouldn't be happening. She
couldn't still want him—she mustn't! It was self-
destructive, demeaning . . .

Spluttering, she forced herself to ignore the way her
breasts were peaking beneath his hands, and gasped
out savagely, 'I can believe Olivia hasn't been around
for a week or two—frustration was the only thing that
ever drove you to stoop to touch me!' Or, even more
hurtfully, the need to sire the child the love of his life
was unable to give him.

'Yes. Of course. Olivia.' His hands slid away from
her and he looked at her with anguish in his eyes.
And then it was gone, too quickly for her to hold and
examine it. She stared into the blank blackness of his
gaze, treading water now that the support of his hard
body had been withdrawn. She had expected anger,
or scorn—never anguish, if anguish it had truly been.
And her own eyes were puzzled as he told her, 'Now
that the thing that kept us apart has been acknowl-

edged for the lie that it was, we must discuss the other. Olivia. It is time.' He turned his dark head and began to swim towards the shore. Charley followed thoughtfully, not hurrying.

She was now perfectly prepared to admit that she had never believed him capable of killing his brother—quite regardless of what Olivia thought she knew. She had used the accusation as a smoke-screen, not wanting to let him know that he had broken her foolish heart, preferring to allow him to see her as a woman who put principle before passion, who had ousted the last few vestiges of love and respect for him from her heart because the crime he had committed disgusted her.

And that was the way she had seen herself, she admitted. It had been the only way she had been able to survive the killing hurt of knowing he had never loved her, had only used her.

But discuss Olivia and her part in his life? The very thought of it made her blood run cold. Yet if she refused he might guess... Guess what? she derided herself with tart defensiveness. Nothing. Nothing at all. So she was a normal woman with a normal woman's needs and he was the most attractive devil ever spawned. So she had responded to his touch. So what?

So she would act as if that bit of embarrassment hadn't occurred, she decided as she slid her feet to the sandy bottom and began to walk out of the sea, pushing her dripping hair back from her face. And if he—for the lord only knew what weird reasons—insisted on 'discussing Olivia', then she would grit her teeth and play along. She would show him that she was a completely different woman, cool, moderately sophisticated, and perfectly able to discuss a part of her life that was now firmly relegated to the past.

The devil in question had his back to the sea as he rough-dried his hair, she noted with relief. And, thankfully, he had pulled on his jeans, covering his disgraceful swimming briefs. She wasn't a prude, but really, the brevity of that black thing he'd been wearing was enough to turn a girl's hair white! She wondered if he did it on purpose, if he knew the effect he had on women, then decided it wasn't a subject worth head-room and took the towel he offered as she drew level, covering herself quickly to avoid the raking glance of those sultry eyes.

But he wasn't looking at her; he was fully occupied in pushing his arms into the sleeves of his shirt and calling a teasing response to something one of the young Spanish women had said to him, her dark eyes openly flirtatious beneath a fringe of tangled black curls.

He simply couldn't resist, could he? Charley thought sniffily as she reached for her own cut-offs and T-shirt, dragging them on over her damp swimsuit. And she wasn't annoyed because none of his attention was coming her way. Certainly not! It simply wasn't very good taste on his part to be in-dulging in remarks of a highly personal nature with a stranger on a public beach!

'Ready?' By the time he loomed over her as she was lacing up her light canvas shoes she had calmed down. What did it matter to her what he did? He could shout lewd remarks to all and sundry for all she cared. All she hoped was that she would be around when he got himself arrested!

'Quite.' She struggled to her feet, ignoring his out-stretched hand. She was damned if she'd touch him, ever again.

'I asked Teresa to give us an early lunch. We can find a shady place in the garden this afternoon. We have things to talk about.'

He meant Olivia, she knew he did. But she wasn't going to get her knickers in a twist about it.

'If that's what you want,' she answered sedately as he led the way to the wide, elegant promenade, 'I'm perfectly agreeable.'

She was proud of her coolly assumed dignity, but a bit miffed by his slanting glance of amusement, the way his sensational mouth curled up at the corners, and briefly infuriated by his, 'If I thought you'd be perfectly agreeable to everything I want, I'd die a happy—and fully satisfied—man.'

But her fury didn't last long because he set himself out to be charmingly uncontentious, seating her at a pavement café and ordering *sangría* and then hiring a taxi to take them back to the *casa*, keeping her amused with wicked, purely local anecdotes until she was light-headed with laughter as they entered the huge iron gates.

The *sangría* must have been more potent than she'd thought, laced with more brandy than was usual, she thought as she trotted contentedly beside him into the cool, shadowy hall. For the past hour he had seemed like the man she had fallen in love with all those years ago, and she still wore a stupid smile on her face as Teresa loomed up to meet them, looking as if she'd swallowed a lemon.

'You have a visitor, *señora*. He insisted on waiting. Perhaps you will see what he wants. Tell him you can spare only two minutes. I am ready to serve lunch.'

Charley giggled foolishly. Somehow she couldn't help it. If only Teresa could see how funny she looked, with her mouth all pulled down at the corners and her nostrils flaring like an old war horse! And she was still giggling, despite Sebastian's black frown, when, presumably hearing voices, Greg put his head round one of the doors and grumbled, 'About time, Charley. I've been sitting in this mausoleum for hours. Where have you been?'

CHAPTER FIVE

THAT brought Charley back to her senses with a vengeance. If Greg had appeared on the beach this morning, when she'd been having such a tough time with her emotions, she might have flung herself at him and begged him to take her away from all this. Right this minute. She could almost hear herself telling him that four weeks here, with this devil, was too high a price to pay for a quick divorce, that she would rather wait for another full year—and then some— than be subjected to . . . well, what she had been subjected to.

But, oddly, now he was here, looking every inch what he was—a reliable, feet-on-the-ground small-town accountant—she wished he were a million miles away. And didn't know why.

Teresa had stumped off in a cloud of disapproval and Sebastian had gone very still and silent. Without looking at him, she knew he would be wearing his mask of arrogant disdain. And Charley's face had gone all wooden; it felt like a board.

'Well?' Greg prompted, clearly annoyed. 'Am I not to be introduced?'

His pleasantly craggy face was sweating, Charley noted dispassionately. He looked very uncomfortable in his tweed jacket, grey flannels and neatly tied striped tie. He was a typical Englishman of the staid and stolid variety. He didn't fit in.

Suddenly appalled by the disloyalty of her thoughts, Charley pushed herself into action, skimming across the vast hall, tucking her arm through his and making herself smile. Of course he didn't fit in. Why should he? And her voice was annoyingly shaky as she apologised, 'Forgive me, darling. Seeing you here was such a shock. I'd no idea you were coming.' And was that the truth! Never, in all the time she'd known him, had he been anything other than safely predictable. That was one of the many qualities she admired. Sebastian had put her off the unpredictable for life!

'Yes. Well…' He sounded somewhat mollified, and patted her hand as it lay on his sleeve. 'I decided to take a few days off. There wasn't time to let you know. I've been waiting hours.'

'I'm sorry.' What else could she say? She slicked her tongue over dry-as-dust lips, wondering how on earth she was supposed to introduce her fiancé to her husband! But Greg handled that problem for her, walking over the tiled floor, his highly polished black shoes making echoes, dragging her with him, his hand outstretched.

'You must be Machado. I'm Gregory Wilson. I've no doubt my fiancée told you all about me.'

'Enough.' Sebastian's tone was utterly chilling. Charley shivered and was cross with herself for letting him affect her. But the devil had completely ignored Greg's outstretched hand and his face was almost frighteningly arrogant. And hard. 'And how long do you intend staying in Cadiz, Wilson?'

He had somehow made the question sound like an insult. Charley squeezed Greg's arm reassuringly as he answered stiffly, 'Three or four days. That's if I can find somewhere to stay. Which is why I came straight here. Charley, shall we go and——?'

'You will stay to lunch,' Sebastian cut in with a sudden and utterly surprising silkiness. 'I will arrange your accommodation while my wife asks Teresa to set an extra place at table.' And then he simply walked away, leaving Charley to stare at the proud, retreating back with suspicious eyes.

What was the devil up to now? From his initial re-action to Greg's obviously unwelcome presence she had expected him to toss the poor man out on his neck. Instead——

'Do you think he means I'm to stay here?'

'What?' Charley frowned as Greg interrupted her search for Sebastian's motives. Then shook her head, giving up, because only someone with a first-class honours degree in irrational behaviour would be able to understand what went on inside that devil's head. 'I wouldn't think so, would you? In the circumstances?'

'Perhaps not, though it would save a packet on hotel bills,' he conceded wryly. 'And anyway, you're staying here—"in the circumstances".'

Charley sighed. So that was why he'd dropped everything to come out here, acting completely out of character. She said dully, 'I did explain about that. Anyway, it's not something we can discuss right now.'

'No, of course not. You're quite right. We'll chew it over later, once I'm settled in. When Machado in-vited me to lunch I was about to ask you to help me find somewhere modest. Clean, though—I don't want to be stuck in something squalid. But not over the top, price-wise. We'll get something sorted out straight after lunch—tell him he needn't bother. We can do without his help.'

Which were her own sentiments exactly. Charley's teeth worried at her lower lip. Why had Sebastian's attitude towards Greg undergone such a sudden change? And why was she letting him take charge of her thoughts when she should be thinking only of Greg? she questioned herself tartly. Then she shook her head, as if to clear it, and said softly, 'You must be tired. If you don't know your way about, it can be quite an undertaking to get here, especially as you don't speak the language. Look, sit down while I go and see Teresa about lunch.' She steered him to one of the tall-backed carved chairs which stood sentinel against the walls. 'Though we needn't stay here,' she pointed out, feeling a little brighter. 'We don't have to. There are so many cafés and small restaurants——'

'No.' Greg shook his head, his hands planted squarely on his knees. 'Might as well eat here, since he offered. And you're right, I'm whacked. Besides, why spend money on food if we don't have to?'

'Why indeed?' Charley sniped, and turned quickly on her heels towards the kitchens.

She was finding it difficult to be nice to him, she really was. He shouldn't have turned up like that. It put her in an impossible position. And would he always—whatever the circumstances—put careful expenditure right at the top of his list of priorities?

So she wasn't in the mood to take Teresa's outspokenly exaggerated comments with her usual equanimity when, announcing that Greg would be staying for lunch, she was met with, 'So the little fat man eats with you! Don Sebastian should have thrown him into the street.'

Swallowing the denial that Greg was either fat or little, and the observation that Teresa's girth was three times that of the lunch guest, Charley said with cold dignity, 'My husband has more manners.'

'So!' Teresa pounced, her black eyes glistening. 'You admit Don Sebastian is your husband! Aha! Try to remember it, *señora*. That man peers in a phrase book and points at words and tries to tell me he is your *novio*—he is *loco* and his accent is an insult. I told him so, in his own language—just to show him! I also told him to come back later—much, much later. But he refused.'

Stony-faced, Charley retreated before she lost her temper. Teresa went too far. The situation was too tangled to explain away in a matter of minutes—even if she had wanted to. And had Teresa ever bothered to remind Sebastian that he had a wife when he'd been conducting his affair with Olivia right there in this house? Of course not! There was one rule for men and another for their wives! And what on earth had possessed her to refer to Sebastian as her husband? It wasn't a relationship she wanted to draw attention to, especially as their marriage would soon be legally over.

Muttering to herself, she trudged back to the hall and found Greg wandering around. She would like to have escaped, to have taken a shower and changed. But there really wasn't time, and she didn't think she could leave him on his own. And he said, his narrowed eyes on the graceful staircase, 'I've been opening doors and looking in rooms. It's quite some place, isn't it? He must be worth a bit to be able to afford to live here.'

'A bit,' Charley agreed repressively. She had never discussed Sebastian's financial status with Greg. Indeed, she had rarely divulged any information, preferring to forget her disastrous marriage. And didn't Greg realise he was being impossibly rude—peering round doors in someone else's home? And didn't he feel uncomfortable with the situation?

Apparently not, because as Sebastian appeared—showered and changed into cool white trousers and a black shirt in a design and fabric that positively flowed, making him look quite stunningly male when, if life were fair, it should have made him look effete—Greg became quite oily.

And life wasn't fair, Charley mourned as Sebastian, putting on a show of exaggerated politeness, led them to the lunch table out in the courtyard. Sebastian had them both at a disadvantage. He looked cool, fantastic and in control while she was still wearing her old cut-offs and unremarkable T-shirt, her skin still feeling sticky with sea-water. And Greg, if anything, looked worse. He was obviously stifling in his tweed sports jacket and flannels, his forehead was dewed with sweat, his short wiry brown hair clung damply to his skull and his neck was definitely red.

And throughout the meal Sebastian watched them both and there was something in his eyes—something unreadable but definitely there—that made him look like a man who was conducting an amusing experiment.

Charley didn't like it. She didn't know what he was up to and she didn't trust him.

'I must say, Machado, it's very civil of you to give me such a splendid lunch—the stranger at your door, and all that. Very civil indeed!' Greg said, and Charley cringed with embarrassment as he laughed at his own feeble joke.

Although she knew he would have much preferred roast beef and Yorkshire pudding and a pint of beer, he had eaten everything in sight and made heavy inroads into the *fino*. And now his tongue seemed to be running away with him.

'But we're both civilised men, I hope; Charley needn't be a bone of contention. No, not at all. After all, you've been apart for four years, so there can't be any bad feeling.'

'Charlotte has now returned,' Sebastian said with a slow, disarming smile, leaning back, idly twisting the stem of his glass this way and that.

Charley could have hit him. He was behaving badly, like a spoilt but charming child, and when Greg shot her a scowling look she said tightly, 'He's playing games. Take no notice.'

'Games?' Greg's scowl deepened and just as suddenly disappeared as he added in a quick low whisper, 'He probably doesn't grasp the finer points. Foreign language, and all that.' And before Charley could tell him that Sebastian had a perfect grasp of English, Greg was launching forth, loudly and slowly, 'I know, old man, but only for four——'

'I asked Andrés to bring the car to the front at three,' Sebastian interrupted silkily. 'It's almost that now.' He rose to his feet, and Charley shuddered as she watched all that insolent grace and saw the beautiful mouth curve in a meaningless smile. 'Shall we find your luggage? Andrés will take you to your hotel.' He named the most prestigious and expensive hotel in the city, those sultry eyes narrowing in dark mockery as he watched Greg struggle to his feet.

'Very civil of you!' Greg puffed, running a finger around the inside of his shirt collar. 'I left my case in the hall. Come along, Charley, don't want to keep the driver waiting.'

She stared at him with blank golden eyes. He wouldn't look so pleased with himself when he was presented with his bill at the end of his stay. He thought Sebastian was bending over backwards to be helpful, that he, Gregory Wilson, was in control of the delicate situation, had come out on top. Little did he realise! In giving the other man any hospitality at all, in allowing him to step a foot inside the house, Sebastian was simply sitting back and allowing Greg to dig his own grave with his shortcomings.

And as an exercise in pure deviousness, it seemed to be working. Looking at Greg, she could suddenly find nothing to like.

'Charlotte has an appointment this afternoon.'

She had been too deep in her own thoughts to be aware of the pregnant silence; it seemed that only Sebastian's shiveringly sexy voice had the power to penetrate the concentration of her thoughts. She blinked, beginning to push herself to her feet, but Sebastian made a wide, flat gesture with one hand, and she, like a puppet, subsided again.

'And naturally, you'll need time to settle in.' Sebastian was metaphorically herding Greg in the direction he meant him to go. But it was patently obvious that Greg couldn't see it. Were his wits too addled by the greedy amount of food and wine he had taken to understand what was happening? For the moment she despaired of him, and relinquished him to his fate when he nodded in complete agreement.

'Quite. It's been a taxing day—especially the journey between Jerez and Cadiz. I'll probably take a shower and catch forty winks. I'll see you this evening, Charley. I'll get in touch when I'm rested.'

She didn't answer, and watched Sebastian usher him away, heard him say, 'Don't phone us; we'll phone you.'

And she could hardly believe Greg's gullibility—or was it a perverted type of arrogance?—as he replied, all affable innocence, 'I'd appreciate that, old man. I believe the Spanish phone system takes some getting used to.'

Did he really believe Sebastian would contact him by phone and tell him that Charley was ready and waiting to go out on the town with him, probably sending a car to collect him? Was he that stupid?

With a gesture of annoyance, Charley shot to her feet and made a hurried departure for her room. She had had no wish whatsoever to spend the afternoon with Greg, watching him explode with horror when he discovered the expensive opulence of the hotel Sebastian had booked him into. Greg wasn't short of money, by any standards, but he hated to part with it unnecessarily. But she didn't want to spend more time with Sebastian, either. Suddenly, she wanted nothing to do with either of them.

A shower helped, and she felt cooler and fresher as she padded back into the opulently decadent bedroom and flung open the door of the massive wardrobe, pulling a face at the serviceable and dull garments she'd brought with her. Then, feeling strangely guilty, she riffled through the clothes she

had left behind when she'd walked out all that time
ago.

None of the expensive dresses or separates would
fit her now. But... Unerringly, her fingers walked
over satins and silks, lace and velvet and linen, and
fished out a diaphanous négligé, part of one of the
many sets of seductive nightwear she'd bought to make
Sebastian see her as a fully adult and sensuous woman
on the occasions when he bothered to spend the night
with her.

She had never got round to wearing this one, and
as she slipped her arms into the wide, floating sleeves
and felt the cool drift of aqua-green silk touch her
body she felt curiously, vibrantly alive. Very much a
woman. Wrinkling her nose, she knotted the tie belt
around her waist and walked over to the tall windows
to close the shutters, blocking out the harsh
Andalucían afternoon light. And heard the whispering silk of the long full skirts as she moved, and
knew Greg wouldn't approve of such a frivolous
garment.

She wished he hadn't taken it into his head to come
out here—for more reasons than one. Leaving aside
the fact that his unexpected arrival had put her in an
almost impossible situation—and surely a more sensi-
tive man would have simply booked himself into an
hotel and then phoned her to say he was here—
Sebastian had made her see him with fresh eyes,
putting the other man into a situation which had dis-
played both his greed and his insensitivity.

Annoyed with herself for thinking that way, she
took a deep breath and promised herself that she
wouldn't give either one of them another thought for
the rest of the afternoon. She would relax, try to
unwind. With the louvres closed, the room was like

an underwater cave. Peaceful. Sinking down on to the huge, soft bed, she closed her eyes and opened them with a snap as Sebastian said, 'You look so comfortable, I think I'll join you.'

'Did nobody ever teach you how to knock?' Charley hoisted herself up on one elbow, the tranquillity of the afternoon shot to pieces, and watched with golden hostility the amused direction of his dark gaze then clutched furiously at the open edges of the négligé which had obviously gaped so revealingly during her recent squirmingly angry moments.

'At the door to my wife's bedroom?' He loped across the room, his eyes lifting from her white-knuckled fingers as they clutched at the fine fabric clothing her breasts to her flushed and furious face. 'Come, come, my little pigeon, you must try to relax.'

'With you around—you must be joking! And don't call me that.' Once, a lifetime ago, or so it seemed, he had called her his little pigeon. She had imagined it to be a term of endearment. Knowing what she now knew, she knew differently. And one raised black brow drew an unthinking explanation. 'You saw me as something plump and grey and six-a-penny. Well, I'm not like that any more.'

It couldn't be a reflection of pain that narrowed his eyes and made his mouth go hard. The light coming into the room was dim, made soft and green by the louvres, and he was certainly still in his irritatingly esoteric mood as he confidently perched himself on the edge of her bed and told her, 'You were certainly never six-a-penny. In fact you were, and are, unique.' His dark eyes glimmered. 'You may have shed your delightful pigeon plumpness, but the curves are still all there, as exciting as ever.' As if to demonstrate his point a hand lifted lazily, and slowly, oh, so slowly, he shaped each breast in turn, his hooded eyes following the movement of his fingers as if he were imprinting every last detail of the size, the shape, the weight and increasing, shaming hardness of each on his mind.

Charley held her breath as her heart fluttered impotently in her chest. She couldn't breathe, she couldn't speak, she couldn't move, because she was loving every second of this erotic exploration, loving it, and at the same time feeling painfully ashamed of herself, knowing she shouldn't be letting him do this to her.

And when his hand at last dropped away she didn't know whether her sigh was one of relief or aching disappointment. But through her confusion she detected a hateful gleam of triumph in his eyes and loathed herself, both for what she had allowed him to do and for the way her breasts were wantonly peaking, pushing against the filmy fabric of her robe.

And loathed him, too, when he casually swung his long legs up on to the bed and rested his back against one of the posts at the foot, watching her with alarmingly narrowed eyes.

The soft green light, the huge and opulent bed, the—the thing she was wearing, the searing recollection of the way he had made her feel when he'd touched her, all added up to an impossibly intimate situation. She glared at him, trying to make herself forget the way her body had become so tinglingly alive, and growled, 'What do you think you're doing? Go away!'

The look he gave her was unnerving in its cynicism, his beautiful voice cool as he reminded her, 'As I told that unimpressive little man, you had an appointment this afternoon. With me, as it happens. Don't try to pretend you've forgotten we'd agreed to talk. I had suggested a shady spot in the garden, remember? However, since you obviously preferred the...comfort?...of your room, I'm not objecting.'

Too right, he wasn't! Charley's face went red. And he was putting this situation down to her! Was he suggesting that she'd deliberately chosen to close the blinds, drape herself in almost transparent silk and lounge around on the bed, waiting for him because she'd known he would come? Was that why he'd touched her? Because he thought she expected it? Oh, shades of the past, indeed—it was humiliating!

'There's nothing to talk about,' she said sulkily. 'There's no point in raking over the past when the future's all settled.'

'With that dreadful little man? Oh, Charlotte—I really don't think so. Do you?'

She wasn't answering that. She scrunched herself up against the pillows, as far as she could get from him, tucking her legs beneath her, making herself as small as she could get, making sure no edges came adrift as she moved.

'Besides, you owe me. After the thing you accused me of, you owe me.' His tone was softly sinister, as if warning her he would take no arguments, take no prisoners in a battle he thought was right.

And perhaps he was right, she thought on a silent inward sigh. The stern and arrogant pride that was so much a part of his character would have made the accusation of murder—a crime committed sneakily, for financial gain, and not in an open, passionate rage—doubly insulting to a man of his qualities.

'So what do you want me to say?' She braced herself, forcing herself to return his steady, unblinking gaze. 'I'll apologise again, if you want me to.'

'No. Tell me what you were told. Exactly what you were told.'

Why? Because it still hurt him to know that Olivia had lied about such a thing? He had told her that the other woman hadn't been in Cadiz, to his knowledge, for a long time. She hadn't believed him, but now, flinching from the bleakness in his black eyes, she did. Had he cut Olivia out of his life because she had lied, his pride proving stronger than sexual obsession? Did he still miss her, ache for her, even so?

'Very well. If it helps you——' she offered, but he cut across her, his voice tight and hard.

'It may. In any case, I need to know. It could alter the perspective.'

On what? She felt too drained to ask, and said in a voice that sounded lost, 'You were away.' And didn't bother to add that although he made a great many business trips he always made sure he was around when Olivia visited. But that time, he hadn't. 'Olivia...' God, how difficult it still was to say that woman's name out loud. She tried to inject strength into her faltering voice. 'Olivia was here. She said she thought I ought to know that you had killed your brother. On the death of your father everything had gone to Fernando. You wanted control—everything. You were ruthless enough to kill to get what you wanted. She said she was warning me.' She shuddered, remembering her shock, her utter disbelief at the time. And tried to put it out of her mind. Just as long as she didn't have to tell him what else Olivia had said.

She simply couldn't bring herself to talk about it, even now, when it was buried deeply in the past, when her besotted love for Sebastian no longer existed, her future with Greg was settled. And it was settled, of course it was.

'And you believed her?' he probed insistently, and she shrugged.

'I don't know.' How shameful that sounded. How disloyal to the man she had loved. Yet she had had to believe it. It had been the perfect excuse. She could never have told him the truth. Knowing he had taken all that blind adoration, the depth of her love, and used it against her, cheating on her, sharing her bed for one reason only, had been a terrible burden to bear. She had needed to walk away from their marriage, keeping some dignity. Had that been such a terrible thing to do?

Yes, perhaps it had been. Perhaps it had been inexcusable. But before the thought could take real root in her brain she said quickly, 'She said that if I had any doubts I should consult the newspapers of the time. You were away, as I said. I went back to London and read the reports. It was all there. The car at the foot of the cliffs and your brother dead inside it. The missing ignition key. The suspicion of foul play, but no proof. Your sudden return to Spain. Olivia filled in the gaps. You were in Plymouth streamlining the import end of the business there. She was to be the new manager, promoted to take the place of the former inefficient one who had been offered early retirement. She had inherited a cottage further along the coast; you were both staying there with her. Fernando had been crazy about her, and showing it openly, and you were jealous...' She caught herself up quickly, gnawing at her lip, feeling his icy gaze. 'Jealous of Fernando's power in the company,' she amended. 'Under the terms of your father's will he inherited everything and you were just a hired hand.'

'Don't stop there,' he commanded drily, his eyes never leaving her troubled face. She gathered herself. Repeating Olivia's lies made her feel dreadful. How could she even have pretended to herself that she believed them?

'The day it happened, it was a Sunday,' she went on woodenly. 'You and Fernando had gone to the offices. She'd followed—I've forgotten what for. She overheard you quarrelling. She heard Fernando say, "You'd be a happy man if I dropped down dead. You'd get the lot. I'd like to be around to see you make an even bigger mess. But you can't have it both ways." Or words to that effect. It's been a long time.' It had, but she still remembered every last poisonous word. 'She also mentioned she'd heard you threaten to kill him.'

'So I had,' Sebastian admitted bleakly. 'But not in any real context. He had just confessed the extent of the mess he'd got the company into. I'd known it had gone downhill after Fernando had taken over, but I hadn't known the depth of the mire we were in. I'd said that I could kill him for his mishandling of the business—anger speaking, nothing else—and went on to say he was going to have to leave all the major decisions to me in future, stop spending a small fortune on his women, his gambling and all the other pleasures he believed he couldn't live without. He had already told me...' Self-castigation was evident in the bitter line of his mouth. But he shook his head, asking her, 'So what else was said to make you believe that I, your husband, could have stooped to murder?'

She deserved the harsh look that accompanied the question, but the business about the missing ignition key had been the most damning. She shivered, and her voice sounded thick as she told him, 'She said that when your brother's car was recovered there was no sign of the ignition key, which pointed, of course, to someone else being involved. Olivia found it in your possession—the key-ring it was on was quite unmistakable. She said Fernando had left in a towering rage and you'd followed him in your own car, persuaded him to stop, then fed him on brandy, pocketed the key and, before Fernando had time to realise what was happening, you'd pushed the car over the edge. She'd got rid of the key for you; she told me that you and she were the only people who knew what had happened.'

'How inventive.' He looked almost pleased, and she stared at him in bewilderment. Of course there had to be some other explanation for the missing key. But she wouldn't have thought it possible that hearing the true extent of Olivia's lies would have brought him anything other than the deepest pain. After all, they had been lovers for years, had intended to marry eventually.

'Of course you didn't take that key,' she said, her voice softening with unwilling compassion, her eyes going very wide when he told her,

'But I did. You were told enough of the truth to tie in with the reports you read, and enough lies to force you to believe the worst. If you had read later reports you would have learned that, following the post-mortem and inquest, a verdict of accidental death was brought in. I gave evidence, repeated what I had already told the police—that, knowing he had had too much to drink, I'd followed him when he'd left the offices, caught up with him when he pulled off at the look-out point on the headland, and tried to persuade him to let me drive him the rest of the way to Olivia's cottage, where we were staying. I said that he refused to budge, but told me he wasn't going to drive any further. To make sure he didn't, I took the key from his ignition and drove back to town, intending to give it back later, when I returned to the cottage that evening, believing he would have sobered up by then. Everything I told them was the truth, but not all the truth. My brother committed suicide.'

His voice held the dreadful ring of conviction, and Charley bit back the instinctive words of sympathy. He wouldn't want to hear them, not from her. Somehow, over the years, he had come to terms with his brother's death, with the way she had walked out on their marriage, accusing him of a dreadful crime. But she did say, and that very quietly, 'So Olivia didn't dispose of "the evidence".'

'Of course not. She knew I had the key because I told her. I took it to the police as soon as I heard what had happened. What I have never told a living soul was that Fernando was threatening suicide. The business was on the verge of bankruptcy—that row Olivia partly overheard was part of his threats; he taunted me with not caring, said I'd be a happy man if he dropped down dead. And I rubbed the poor sod's nose in it, laying down the law, telling him he'd have to hand over control to me, stop living the life of a millionaire!' He swung his long legs off the bed and began to pace the room.

Charley shivered, hugging her arms around her body. She said, 'Don't blame yourself,' but he didn't hear her.

'I didn't take him seriously. I thought it was the alcohol talking. He'd had far too much wine with lunch that Sunday and by the time I caught him up at the office he was drinking brandy from the flask he always carried as if it were water. When he stormed out, I had to follow. I was concerned about the amount he'd been drinking. As I told the police, I caught up with him when he pulled on to the view-point. I didn't tell them about the suicide threats. Why should I? Never mind that I hadn't taken them seriously—I know that had he been in his right mind he would have preferred to know that his death would be recorded as an accident rather than suicide—implying the lack of moral strength to face up to a mess of his own making. I didn't argue when the police decided he'd tried to drive back to the cottage, reaching for the ignition as he released the brakes—it was the sort of thing any man with as much alcohol in his blood as he'd had could have done.'

'Sebastian!' Charley couldn't bear it. He looked like a man in torment. She swung her legs off the bed in a flurry of silk and padded over the floor, resting her head against the wide rigidity of his shoulderblades and twining her arms around his waist. 'You mustn't blame yourself for what happened,' she whispered, her heart aching for him, for the wicked accusations she'd been so ready to hurl at him all those years ago, hiding behind them because she hadn't been strong enough to let him know the whole truth. 'And perhaps the police were right; perhaps it was an accident.'

'Who knows?' His warm hands covered hers, gripped them. 'I have my own opinions, but, in the end, who really knows the truth?' He swung round within the fragile circle of her arms, his hands pulling her head down against his chest. 'It's something I've come to terms with.' He tilted her chin, forcing her head back, and she saw the glitter of his eyes and stopped breathing, her heart tumbling about beneath her ribs. And his voice was a low caress of dark enchantment as he murmured, 'I understand what happened. I forgive you now. Your apologies are accepted.'

His lips against hers were hard and hot as he smothered her mouth with rapid kisses, making her head spin. What was he trying to do, to say? She couldn't think straight, and his powerful body was burning hers through her thin covering of silk. She could barely stand upright for the fluid desire that was coursing so hotly through her veins.

She had to put a stop to it right now. Now, before her resolve dissolved entirely in this heady rush of need, this aching, terrible wanting. Charley groaned as he threaded his fingers through her hair, positioning her mouth to receive the continuing seductive onslaught of those devastating kisses, and pushed at him with ineffectual fists, twisting her head away from that marauding mouth, her voice a strangled croak as she pleaded, 'Don't! Oh, don't! Oh, I don't understand!'

'I do.' He dipped his head to recapture her mouth, the tip of his tongue sliding over her rosy, parted lips, and she shuddered helplessly, clinging to him because her body had gone boneless. 'And that's all that matters.' His tongue delved more deeply and Charley whimpered fretfully, her fingers digging into the hard muscles of his shoulders.

Her body was betraying her, denying her mind any control, and her attempt to fight back was too feeble for words; she admitted that much because when she managed thickly, 'You arrogant bastard!' he merely conceded, his black eyes glittering,

'If this is arrogance, then why don't we both enjoy it? Stop thinking, pull the shutters down on that contentious brain of yours, and simply feel. Feel this, and this . . .' He slid his hands beneath the silky robe, cupping her breasts, then dipped his dark head to suckle possessively at the swollen peaks, his voice richly appreciative as he murmured against her burning flesh, 'Let your body do the thinking; it does it so beautifully.' One careless movement disposed of the tie belt around her waist, and as the cloud of aqua silk drifted its treacherous way to the floor to pool around her feet Charley knew she had lost the battle and didn't care.

And when he scooped her into his arms she had lost the very last vestige of self-preservation, her body warm and submissive, and when he whispered, 'Come with me to the marriage bed, where you belong,' she simply gave in to the sensuous temptation that was Sebastian Machado, twined her arms around him, and buried her face in the hard curve of his neck, her tongue lapping the slightly salty, close-grained masculine skin as he carried her to the vast, luxuriously decadent four-poster.

CHAPTER SIX

IT WAS like floating in a warm dark sea of pure sensation, Charley thought, her head whirling, her breath a ragged, wantonly revealing gasp as Sebastian joined her in the deep feather-down softness, his naked body hard with primitive masculine arousal, a shimmer of sweat on the hair-roughened olive-toned skin.

'*Querida* . . .' His voice was ravaged, torn from him as he moulded her body with possessive hands, his hooded eyes following every movement of his fingers until her flesh ached for him and she writhed beneath his touch, arching her back, turning, rubbing against him, her own hands wild as they tried to discover every last inch of his tormentingly masculine body. There was an explosive surge of need inside her that she was too intoxicated by desire to try to understand.

Certainly, it was new to her. Never before, even at her most besotted, had she taken the initiative; she had been overawed, submissive, too shy to make demands . . .

Something had happened to her in the intervening years, she thought muzzily as she covered his wide chest with avidly moist kisses, following him, her body cleaving to his as he rolled over on to his back, his thick lashes twin black crescents that softened the harsh lines of his cheekbones as he unwittingly gave her the explanation, his voice sultry with desire. 'You have grown up, *cariña*. See what you do to me.'

Grown up? Charley held her breath and went very still. Her skin was suddenly cold, as if a blast of arctic air had cut through the drowsy heat of the Andalucían afternoon. Hadn't her pride in her emerging maturity of outlook been her greatest consolation during the past four years? Was she now about to throw away all that painfully acquired ability to turn the key on the past, to grow into the independent, clear-seeing woman she wanted to be, to forget the girl who had been nothing more than a besotted doormat?

Was she?

Could she allow this man to make love to her, to enslave her all over again? Was she willing to let that happen, knowing that Greg was barely a mile away? Could she jeopardise the future she had made for herself because Sebastian had decided he wanted to make love to her?

'No!' she uttered bleakly as she twisted away, evading the erotic punishment of his hands.

For punishment it was; she saw that very clearly now. Quickly she turned her eyes from his anguished face. Frustrated lust could be painful, she granted him that. She wasn't going to let herself care.

'Charlotte...' He pulled himself up on his elbows, rolling over on to his side as she dragged the top cover around her shaking body. She shook her head savagely.

'Don't say anything. It was a nice try, but it didn't work.' And saw his face go hard.

Standing, she discovered her legs felt as insubstantial as water vapour and wondered if she'd be able to cover the distance to the bathroom without falling in a heap. That would be the final shame, the last dreadful ignominy.

'Where are you going?'

His voice was harsh and she answered tightly, 'To shower.' To scrub every last trace of him from her skin. 'I don't want to see you here when I've finished. Don't expect me back for dinner; I'm going to see Greg.'

'Ah.' Devil's eyes glimmered at her between thick black lashes as he swung on to his back again, his arms folded behind his head. 'At what point, I wonder, did you remember he existed?'

He actually had the gall to smile, a slow curving of sensuous lips that made her grind her teeth, reinforcing her opinion that he had decided to seduce her out of a cold, harsh need for revenge.

Hadn't he told her that because of the accusation of cold-blooded fratricide she had levelled at him four years ago he had vowed to have revenge, to make her taste the kind of pain that turned the soul to iron? That, to that end, he had spent lavishly to have her watched, her every movement reported back to him, biding his time? And now the time had come.

Dragging her eyes from his mesmeric gaze, she compressed her mouth and walked away, shivering as his silky-soft words followed her.

'Fly, little pigeon. I am content to wait.'

And what did he think he meant by that? Charley wasn't going to ask. He could be as enigmatic and irritating as he liked. She didn't care. She hated him!

She stayed under the shower until she felt saturated, half expecting to hear him hammer on the door. The silence was unnerving, her thoughts even more so. She'd been such an utter fool. The love she had once had for him had long since gone, but the sexual chemistry was still there, stronger than ever if her un-inhibited response was anything to go by.

It was demeaning.

Drying her hair took next to no time, and as she flicked the comb through the sleek short style she realised her hands were trembling, and tried to get a grip on herself. She had allowed her body to respond to the uniquely potent masculinity of his, to the inti-macy of the situation—but how many women could have resisted? Besides, the fact and the manner of his brother's death still had the power to affect him deeply, despite the way he'd told her he'd come to terms with it. She wouldn't have been human if she hadn't felt some stirrings of compassion, hadn't of-fered what comfort she could.

But the excuses did little to comfort her, and her golden eyes were apprehensive as she wrapped a smothering bath-sheet around her slender body and braced herself to walk back into the bedroom, more than half expecting to see him still lying on the bed, despite her earlier strictures. But thankfully the room was empty, and she expelled a long sigh of relief before dragging her clothes on—the black skirt and cream blouse—and stuffing her feet into sandals.

Her nervous haste to get away from this house made her clumsy, and she growled with annoyance as she dropped her lipstick and watched it roll out of sight beneath an awesomely carved chest of drawers.

Leave it.

She would rather meet Greg wearing no make-up at all than run the risk of Sebastian coming back into the room. Besides, Greg wasn't the type to criticise her appearance. He never seemed to notice what she was wearing; he didn't mind how she looked.

At the dog-end of siesta time the house was re-assuringly silent, and she made it to the street without encountering another soul and hurried down the length of it, her spine prickling with apprehension, half expecting Sebastian to follow, to attempt to force her back.

She couldn't understand why he had allowed her to get away, particularly when she'd told him she was going to Greg. Quite sure now that his attempt at se-duction—and, let's face it, it had very nearly been successful—had been fuelled by his need for revenge, she couldn't understand why he had given in so easily. He had meant to hurt her, to give her the kind of pain that she would never forget, of that she was certain. It wasn't as if he really wanted her, or felt anything for her, was it? He would have contacted her years ago if he had. He had never wanted her, only the child he had expected her to give him. He had always loved Olivia.

No, the devil had wanted to make love to her until she became addicted, reduce her to the level of a be-sotted doormat all over again, ruin her relationship with Greg, and then throw her out. So why had he let her walk away? She would never understand him, not if they both lived to be a thousand years old!

As she reached the imposingly elegant façade of the hotel Greg was using she made a determined effort to put Sebastian and what had happened right out of her mind. She owed it to Greg, and to herself. But when the receptionist she spoke to directed her to his room she shook her head, preferring to send up a message, and sat down in the luxurious, marble-floored foyer to wait.

'You could have come up.' Greg looked as if he had only just woken, his face puffy from sleep, his tone enough to make Charley feel both guilty and selfish. But, for a reason she couldn't explain, not even to herself, she felt reluctant to be alone with him.

'But there's so much to do and see here in Cadiz,' she returned, standing, tucking her arm through his. 'We shouldn't waste a moment as you'll be here for such a short time.' Did that sound as if she were trying to get him back to England with indecent haste? she wondered, frowning at her lack of tact. And offered quickly, 'I know a bar where we can get a really good cup of tea, and that's not easy, I promise you!'

But not even that offer, delivered in her bounciest tone, could bribe the sulkiness from his mouth. And the reason became predictably apparent when he grumbled as they negotiated the impressive steps down to street level, 'I'm booking out of here first thing in the morning. I nearly had a stroke when I read the tariff! I can't think why Machado booked me into the place.'

I can, Charley thought, her mouth going tight. Sebastian had gleaned enough information on Greg to know how he hated to spend money. But she pushed evil thoughts of thumbscrews and boiling oil to the back of her mind and said, 'Down here. And afterwards we can walk on the promenade—or sightsee, whichever you prefer. There are so many beautiful churches and interesting museums and——'

'It's far too hot,' Greg objected, and Charley bit back the obvious retort that he should have left his tweed sports jacket behind, changed into something cooler and more casual. But if he was determined to be fractious, then she was just as determined to be nice to him, even though her motives were flawed, stemming from all that undislodgeable guilt over the way she had behaved with Sebastian, she acknowledged uncomfortably.

The small pavement café she remembered from her earlier days in the city was just as she remembered it. And they still served what Greg pronounced 'a decent cup of English tea', their prices modest enough to satisfy even him.

'Better now?' She wrinkled her neat nose at him, smiling over the rim of her glass, preferring freshly squeezed orange juice herself, served with plenty of ice. And he grinned sheepishly back at her, taking her hand across the table.

'Sorry I was such a grouch. Only we're going to have to find me somewhere else to stay. I don't see the sense in paying those prices just for a place to sleep. I can kip down anywhere, provided it's clean and reasonably comfortable.'

'Of course,' Charley replied absently, dragging a deep breath into her lungs and expelling it shakily.

His smile, his touch, did nothing to her. She wondered now if it ever had. Had she agreed to marry him only because she believed, at some deep and vulnerable level, that she was missing out on the securities and comforts of a home of her own, a man of her own, a family? Had her hard-won metamorphosis made her forget all the pagan splendour, the sheer heart-stopping ecstasy, of loving a man until it filled her heart and mind and body to the exclusion of all else?

Could she ever respond to Greg as she had responded so recently to Sebastian? She didn't know, but she didn't think so. No, no doubt about it, she probably wouldn't be able to respond to Greg at all!

She twisted uncomfortably in her seat, her face flushing as she remembered her utterly, unforgivably wanton behaviour in the huge bed less than a couple of hours ago.

She had never made love with Greg, using her married status as an excuse, and although he hadn't been exactly over the moon about her embargo he had respected her wishes, contenting himself—if that was the word—with the type of kisses and mild caresses she had found comforting at best, and tiresome if she hadn't been in the mood to be touched.

'You look very hot,' Greg's voice impinged. 'You should have had a cup of tea. It's much more cooling and thirst-quenching than any amount of cold stuff— it's a proven fact.'

'Oh, is it!' If he said that tea was cheaper, too, she would scream.

Charley closed her eyes, immediately regretting the way she had snapped. He had irritated her from the moment of his arrival, and it wasn't getting any better. She didn't know what was happening to her. And Greg said, sounding as if he were accusing her of something underhand, 'You didn't tell me that Machado is an extremely wealthy man.'

'Should I have done?' Charley didn't know what Sebastian's financial status had to do with anything, and her blank expression seemed to put him in a better humour.

'You need a keeper, sweetheart!' He beckoned the waiter, pointed at his empty cup, and instructed, '*Dos, por favor*,' at the top of his voice, as if the poor man were deaf, looking pleased with himself as he closed his phrase book. 'Of course you should have told me.' He leaned over the table, his voice low, as if afraid of being overheard. 'It could make a considerable difference. Quite a considerable difference, in fact. You never told me much about him; I always imagined him to be some type of hobo, one of the great low-paid. But one glimpse of that house he lives in— the style he lives in, if that lunch was anything to go by, not to mention the car that took me to the hotel— got me thinking. So when I checked in at Reception I got talking to the head man—thankfully, he does have some English—and made a few enquiries. Machado, it seems, is much respected hereabouts, owns one of the most financially successful export companies in the country. You could claim a nice fat settlement——'

'You think so?' Charley butted in bleakly. She had never wanted anything from Sebastian, only his love. As he had been incapable of giving that, she wanted nothing.

'I don't just think so—I know so!' He scowled at the waiter as he brought the fresh tea to their table. 'Good lord, woman, you could have been receiving hefty maintenance payments for years! I don't know why you separated—you never did tell me the details—but, having met him, and knowing you as well as I do, I'd stake my life on its being all his fault.'

He pushed her tea over the table and she stared at it, frowning. She didn't want it. And Greg was telling her, 'We're going to have to get a good lawyer on to it the moment we get back to England. Forget about a divorce this year—let him drag it out as long as he likes. I can wait.' He ran an impatient finger round the inside of his collar. 'We'll both head home tomorrow and get wheels turning. We'll take him for every penny we can, and then some, and——'

'No,' Charley stated, her voice coldly emphatic. 'I want nothing from him. Nothing.' Not even his love-making? a snide little voice prompted inside her head, and she shook it to dispel the unwelcome truth, and tried to concentrate on Greg. But no matter how hard she tried she couldn't recapture that feeling of warm companionship. How could she ever have contemplated marrying him? Had she really been so lonely, so desperate for her own home, her own family?

Coming back to Cadiz, seeing Sebastian again, wanting Sebastian again, had made her see herself and her relationship with Greg in an entirely new light. Had opened her eyes to the truth.

The sexual magic, the feeling of being drawn to and bound to just one man, was still there, as undiminished and untarnished as on the day she had first met her husband. And at some level of consciousness she must have known it, right from the moment he had stepped out of the shadows in the great hall to meet her.

And there was more, she recognised with a sense of hopelessness. She still loved him. She had tried to deny it, but what else could explain her acceptance of his insistence that she stay with him for the period he had stipulated, the utter repugnance she felt as Greg made his greedy plans to bleed the other man for all he could get?

Bleakly, she raised her eyes to Greg. He seemed to be having difficulty keeping his temper. She wondered why his first marriage had broken up, but wasn't interested enough to try to find out. And she re-

peated, knowing this was the end for them, the end
of a cosy and comfortable illusion, 'No.'

'Now listen, sweetheart.' He was having to struggle
to keep his voice calm, she noted dispassionately,
wondering how she was going to tell him it was all
over—the wedding plans, their hopes for the future.
Everything. In the end she didn't have to think about
it, because when he fixed a smile on his face and told
her, 'I know you're the least mercenary soul alive,
and that's one of the things I've always admired about
you, but you don't want to be taken for a fool, do
you? He owes you, and I'm going to see you collect—
you can safely leave that side of it to me if you're
squeamish about it. Just think of the difference it
could make to our future,' she replied, without having
to think about it at all,

'We no longer have a future together. I'm sorry.'

But she wasn't sorry. All at once she felt as light
as air. Free. How could she have ever believed they
could have made a comfortable, companionable life
together when the very sight of him now put her teeth
on edge?

At the moment he was looking stunned, and
Charley felt the first, admittedly small, stirrings of
self-disgust. She could have broken it more gently,
with more kindness, could have remembered their
former friendship and allowed it to soften her attitude.

Yet how could she tell him that the past few hours
had opened her eyes to character traits that she had
either overlooked or made excuses for in the past?
That she had finally seen him for what he was: ped-
antic, mean and greedy? She wasn't prepared to hurt
him that much.

'I don't know what you're talking about,' Greg stated at last, looking and sounding more annoyed than upset. 'Why shouldn't we have a future together? That's what I'd like to know. We did have until ten minutes ago!'

'Greg...' Her fingers traced patterns on the table-cloth. 'It just wouldn't work. Marriage. We don't love each other. We'd end up making each other miserable.'

Love had never been mentioned on either side. Not once. They had just somehow—and inexcusably, she saw now—drifted into the acceptance that they would marry when she was free, make a life together. She knew now that it could never be enough, probably not for him and certainly not for her. Knowing what love really was, she could settle for nothing less.

Greg snorted, his face going redder, 'And when did you reach that momentous decision? I thought you were adult, but you're acting like a child. There's more to a successful marriage than so-called romantic love. It doesn't last, you know. And when it goes, what are you left with? At least with us we know where we stand.' He leaned forward, making an effort to speak persuasively, trying to smile. 'We like and respect each other, you know we do, sweetheart. We have common goals in life. And when we're married there'll be a lot more. Bed, for instance. I'll make it nice for you...'

'*Nice*'! What she had so recently experienced with Sebastian could hardly be called nice! Explosive, ec-static, earth-shattering... but certainly never as tame as '*nice*'!

'And later on there'll be children, of course. We'd like two, wouldn't we? And with a big fat divorce settlement we can start a family much sooner than we'd originally planned——'

'No!' Charley glowered at him, her face set. 'I'm sorry to have broken it so suddenly, but that's all. Don't ask me to explain; just accept it. It's for the best.'

'In whose opinion?' His lower lip jutted ominously. 'Yours, of course. And you don't have to explain. I can see it all.' There was a white line of temper around his mouth, but Charley faced his outrage, his disgust, because maybe she deserved it, or some of it at least. 'Against all my advice, you came in person to ask for a divorce when everything could have been handled much more smoothly through a solicitor. At the time I couldn't understand why. I can now, though. I didn't know he was as rich as sin. But you did. And you decided to try for a reconciliation. Your earnings are nothing to write home about and I could never give you the kind of lifestyle he could. So you chanced your arm. And he insisted you stay for a few weeks, or no divorce in the immediate future—who's kidding whom? You probably refused to leave and he couldn't be bothered to throw you out. But he will, make no mistake about that! What could a man like that want with a woman like you?' He pushed himself to his feet, the chair scraping over the paving slabs. 'When I think of the money I wasted flying over here, thinking you might need help sorting him out—not to mention the small fortune I'm going to have to shell out for that bloody hotel room!'

He looked as if he were about to explode with fury, but Charley couldn't feel sorry for him. How dared he suggest she'd lied about Sebastian's stipulation? How dared he accuse her of being a gold-digger? She stared at him with cold amber eyes and said dismissively, 'So bill me,' and watched him stalk away in his unsuitable clothes and wondered whether he'd find his way back to his hotel through the warren of narrow streets. And didn't much care.

And felt blithely, wonderfully, ecstatically free! And for a while she sat while the tea went cold, people watching, then paid the bill and wandered aimlessly through the ancient city, soaking up the atmosphere. The streets were coming to life again, the shutters of tiny shop windows being rolled back, the buzz of the ubiquitous Vespinos filling the air, vendors plying their wares—fruit and flowers and vegetables—outside the huge covered market.

She was content, completely at home in the exotic city she had adopted as her own, shutting out all thought and giving herself to each passing moment until, eventually, as dusk closed in, she found a pavement café and ordered salad and *fino*.

Everywhere was bustling, and Charley knew from experience that when the Gaditanos came out for the evening they stayed out. They had an enormous and exuberant capacity for enjoyment. And she still felt part of it. And at last, as so many of the others did, Charley threaded her way through to the wide, elegant stone promenade and walked until her feet ached, then leaned against the coping that topped the carved balusters and listened to the slow withdrawing sigh of the sea as the spent waves sloughed back against the shore.

The promenade was thronged with people enjoying the cool dusk, laughing and chatting in idly strolling groups, and suddenly, for no apparent reason, depression settled around her like a heavy black cloak.

She would have to return to England. There was no reason to stay. It was immaterial now whether

Sebastian agreed to a divorce or not. She wouldn't be marrying Greg, or anyone. She would never be able to love another man, not after Sebastian.

And had Greg been right? Had she insisted on flying out to see her husband in person to ask for a divorce, acting against all reason, because she had been secretly yearning for a reconciliation? Oh, not for the mercenary reasons he had suggested, but because she still loved him more than life? Had she never stopped loving him through all those dark years of separation, even though she'd tried to convince herself that he was guilty of a murder she had always known in her heart that he would have been constitutionally incapable of committing?

It had been such a stupidly histrionic smoke-screen, hiding the truth that couldn't be borne: that he had chosen to marry her to get an heir because the woman he really loved was incapable of bearing children.

And that, at least, hadn't changed. He had taken her, step by painful step, through the time of his brother's tragic death, demanding to know exactly what had been said. But he had said nothing to refute the accusation that at the time of their marriage, and during it, up until—apparently—he had discovered how evilly Olivia had lied, he had been deeply in love with the other woman, using her, plain old Charley, in the cruellest way possible.

No, nothing had changed.

Tears suddenly filled her eyes and she blinked them furiously away. And heard the slam of a car door, heard him call her name, and turned with misery clutching at her heart to face him.

CHAPTER SEVEN

HE WAS standing directly in the pool of light shed by one of the many ornate lamp standards that marched along the top of the stone balustrade, the sleek black shape of the big Mercedes behind him. And the light illuminated every hard line of his satanically beautiful features.

'Get in.'

She'd be a fool to defy the harsh command, the graphically authoritarian gesture of his hand, and although the unexpected sight of him meant her heart was thumping out of control, and left her legs feeling definitely unsteady, Charley walked to the waiting vehicle with her head held high, not looking at him.

He said nothing as he slid in beside her and eased the big car out into the flow of traffic. But the stern remoteness of his strong profile said it all. Sebastian Machado was not amused.

She sat woodenly in the luxuriously upholstered front passenger seat, staring ahead, seeing nothing. The shamefully vivid total recall of the way they had been together in the sumptuous bed warred with the hopeless knowledge of her love for him and the certainty that she must leave tomorrow morning, as early as possible. And she was glad he was maintaining that simmering silence, because even if he had spoken she wouldn't have been able to answer coherently.

She badly needed to cry, but wouldn't let herself. Not now. Time for tears later, for regrets, for the self-

indulgence of all those endless 'if only's. If only he
had once loved her, seen her as anything other than
a healthy nubile body on which to get an heir, if only
he hadn't obsessively loved Olivia and didn't still, in
the bitter core of his heart, regret the inbred fierce
pride that had forced him to sever all connections with
the woman who had spread such infamous lies about
him and the manner in which his brother had died.

But one thing was certain; tomorrow she would
walk away, and this time the parting would be final.
No second chances, no more of the secretly nurtured
hopes she hadn't realised she'd been harbouring, no
more illusions.

She would never see him again.

But she couldn't bear her final memory of him to
be one of aching silence. So she dragged in a tentative
breath and moistened her lips and asked, just for
something to say to break this dreadful silence, 'How
did you find me in all this throng? Or was it coinci-
dence because you weren't really looking?'

'I was looking.'

A sideways, flickering glance revealed the cold twist
of his mouth. And something more: lines of strain
cruelly illuminated by street-lamps and the light from
the dashboard. As if he'd been worried?

Scrub that!

Oh, why did she continually clutch at straws? Did
she really and truly enjoy the bitter taste of self-defeat?
She knew he had never cared about her—and cared
even less than ever now, if that were possible. So why
the hell should he worry?

'You shouldn't have bothered. It's not dreadfully
late,' she returned with a lightness that was hard to
achieve, determined to keep some semblance of civi-

lised intercourse during what must be their final few minutes in each other's company.

But he, obviously, had no such scruples, because his voice was a lash as he threw at her, 'I bothered. I've been scouring the streets for hours looking for you and Wilson. If I'd seen you together I would have known you weren't holed up in his hotel room, carrying on where you'd left off with me. Do you make love to him the way you made love to me?' Not waiting for an answer to his hateful question, he swung the big vehicle into a wickedly narrow street and snapped out another. 'Where is he, anyway?'

Blood boiled in Charley's veins. Oh, what a bastard he was! He actually sounded as if he cared. But of course he cared, she deduced ill-temperedly, putting the tips of her fingers to her temples, where a niggling ache was beginning to pulse. If she and Greg had been in bed together he would have known his sly plans hadn't worked. So to hell with civilised behaviour!

'On his way back to England, for all I know,' she retorted bitterly. 'One way or another you've ruined our relationship. Isn't that what you set out to do?'

There was a slight, almost imperceptible pause, as if he needed a fraction of time to assimilate what she had told him, before he admitted, 'Yes. But don't blame me. The fat man dug his own grave all by himself.' Then he continued suavely, 'I simply put him in a position where his greed and mean-mindedness would hit you between your pretty yellow eyes.'

But you don't know the half of it, Charley decided, gritting her teeth together and closing her eyes wearily against the headache that was getting steadily worse. She wasn't about to tell him that Greg had been practically slavering at the prospect of her wringing a fat packet of alimony from him.

And she certainly had no intention of mentioning the rest of it. She had spent a year of her life letting him know how much she loved him, every glance from her adoring eyes telling him she was his—his to trample on if he so pleased. And he had pleased; oh, boy, how he had pleased! In retrospect her behaviour had been utterly demeaning. She had been so unknowingly trampled upon that it was a wonder she'd ever been able to scrape herself up off the floor!

So never again. Never, never again would she give him the smallest clue to the way she really felt about him.

Jerkily, she expelled the breath she hadn't realised she'd been holding as the car drew to a halt on the main courtyard of the Casa de las Surtidores. The tension headache which had been getting steadily worse ever since she'd entered the car now began to pound without mercy. Yet, perverse devil that he was, Sebastian seemed totally relaxed as he turned to her, sliding an arm along the back of her seat.

All that earlier hard-bitten annoyance had gone, as if it had never been, and his features, washed by the glimmering light of the courtyard lamps, were highlighted by that slow, wicked smile of his.

She didn't trust him an inch. Or herself, when he looked at her that way.

Twisting her head aside, she felt for the door release, wincing as pain stabbed through her temples, and scrambled out of the car, biting her lip as she stumbled. And he was beside her in seconds, and, even though the slam of his door had given her warning, a momentary dizziness left her incapable of moving.

'*Querida*?' He was so very close. She could hear the soft hiss of indrawn breath between his teeth, see the dark concern in his eyes as he gently turned her to face the light, and she cursed herself for her temporary weakness and him for the enormity of his easy charm.

She had meant to walk swiftly into the house, to her room, to start packing ready for an early departure in the morning. Yet here she was, a creature of no will and little substance, her body weakly craving the supporting strength and warmth of his, almost sagging against him as he brushed the pad of one thumb across the hollow beneath one of her cheekbones.

'So pale,' he murmured softly. 'Are you ill, little pigeon?'

'No.'

With an effort, Charley rallied. There was only so much she could take without giving way to the degrading need to rest her aching head against the warm haven of his chest, anchor her arms around his spectacular body, then let the tears fall and surrender herself completely to his will. The temptation was almost too much to withstand, but fight it she must, because if she didn't she would find herself blurting it all out, telling him she still loved him and always would, begging for whatever crumbs he might be able to spare her. Her mouth twisted with violent self-disgust.

'A slight headache, nothing more.' She stepped back decisively, creating an essential distance, then swayed dizzily on her feet as the pain at her temples bit deeply, and he said something profane in a thick, dark voice and scooped her up into his arms and strode towards the house. And didn't stop until he had reached her room, although she did register the terseness of his voice as he barked out a spate of staccato commands to Teresa, who must have been hovering.

The sumptuous bed seemed to reach out to enfold her as he gently laid her down and removed her sandals, but she didn't want him to leave her and had to fight the desperate urge to call him back when he straightened up and walked away.

This was simply awful, she thought miserably, on the brink of tears. Why couldn't she stop loving the wretch? Why had she allowed herself to get into such an emotional mess? And cursed herself all over again for the sweet relief that flowed through every inch of her body as he returned within moments.

'Lie still,' he commanded softly as she tried to force herself up against the pillows, desperately searching for the determination to tell him she was fine now, just fine, and would he please go away. And he calmly reinforced his instruction with the drift of long fingers through her hair as he sat on the bed beside her. His eyes raked her face, the line of the frown between his eyes deepening as he produced a cool damp cloth and gently began to wipe her forehead.

It was soothing, soporific, but she didn't dare relax, and knew she was right to stay on her guard when he informed her drily, 'You're obviously not up to what I had in mind.' His wide shoulders moved in a minimal shrug, his sensual mouth indenting at one corner. 'But tomorrow's another day, isn't it, *querida*?'

She shut out the temptation of that gorgeous mouth by closing her eyes. And she wouldn't even think about whatever it was he had had in mind. And the quaver in her voice was the only indication that his touch, the nearness of him, could affect her in any way as she came back with, 'So it is. I'm leaving tomorrow, so you can stop playing at ministering angels and let me get on with my packing.'

He wouldn't force her to stay if her mind was made up. Why should he? True, she had prevented him taking his attempted seduction to its conclusion, but that would mean little or nothing to him. He could take her or leave her; he wasn't that bothered. He had already achieved what he'd admitted he'd set out to do and ruined her relationship with Greg; that was the important thing, as far as he was concerned, surely?

She had, albeit unwittingly, been the cause of the break-up between him and Olivia when she had opened his eyes to the disgusting lies his lover had told in her successful attempt to get rid of the unwanted wife. So his revenge would have been complete when she'd told him that she and Greg were no longer thinking of marriage. And she expected either an uninterested shrug or a blandly polite offer to drive her to the airport. But what she got was, 'You're going nowhere unless I go with you.'

And her head was aching too much to let her make any sense of that, and his fingers were still gently stroking her forehead, producing a dreadful lethargy. And if he'd meant to say any more, explain what his motives were, he was interrupted by a knock on the door.

It was Teresa, bringing warm milk and a bottle of pain-killers, and she peered at Charley then sniffed, 'You missed dinner. No wonder your head aches. You've no flesh on your bones as it is.' Then to Sebastian, 'And as for you, you should keep a better eye on her! I'll bring up a tray. A nice *tortilla*, perhaps?'

'That will be all, thank you, Teresa.' Sebastian's mouth twitched at the corners, his tone dismissive. 'If the *señora* requires food I'll let you know.'

'If? There should be no ifs about it! I'll...'

But one warning glance from black ice eyes sent the housekeeper stumping out of the room, knowing she'd gone as far as she dared and resenting it. Charley bit worriedly at her lower lip, knowing that after that decisive dismissal Teresa wouldn't be back. Sebastian only tolerated the sharp edge of her tongue, her interference, as long as it amused him and didn't go against his wishes. And having the housekeeper popping in and out of the room was not what he had in mind. For some suspect reason he wanted them to be alone.

The very silence was terrible, the tension inside her almost intolerable, making her feel decidedly ill. But Sebastian seemed unaffected. He was moving around the room with the indolent grace that was such an unmistakable part of him, and she shot him a venomous look, heaved herself up against the heaped pillows, and swung her legs over the side of the bed.

Why couldn't he go away and leave her alone? She would feel better if she could begin to unwind, and how could she hope to do that while he was around?

'Don't look so blighted.' The trace of husky amusement in his voice made her want to spit. What was so all-fired funny?

'You wouldn't be dancing around and grinning if your head hurt,' she informed him, deploring the sulky, defensive note in her voice, peering at him through lowered lashes as he uncapped the bottle and shook two tablets into the palm of his hand.

'Take these. They might make you drowsy, but they'll get rid of the headache.' He passed her the glass of warm milk and dropped the tablets into her other hand. 'Cheer up, I don't think you'll die quite yet.'

'I am perfectly cheerful, thank you,' she grumbled, refusing to rise. And she swallowed the pain-killers with two gulps of milk. Drowsy she could do without. She still had her packing to do. But anything to get rid of him.

Charley put the glass down on the small silver tray, but Sebastian pushed it straight back into her hands.

'Drink all of it. Every last drop.'

Sighing, she lifted the glass to her lips again and drained it. She didn't feel up to fighting him, even though warm milk was quite definitely her least favourite drink. He would stay exactly where he was until she obeyed him, in any case. Defiance simply for the sake of it wasn't worth the aggro. And he took the empty glass from her, his smile annoyingly smug, then turned her world upside-down as he bent his dark head to lap the milky moustache from her upper lip.

At the touch of his tongue against her skin every nerve-end ignited in a fever of spiralling response, her heart nearly heaving itself out of her chest. He only had to touch her to send her wild. And all on their own, her soft, quivering lips parted in blind, unthinking invitation, wanting to feel the sweet invasion of his tongue against hers, her head whirling giddily with the sheer tormenting insistence of her need.

But he didn't take her mouth, and by the time she was sufficiently back in control of herself to realise what he was doing it was almost too late.

'Stop it—I can manage!'

With a supreme effort, she slapped at the hands that were deftly removing her blouse, but his movements didn't falter as he disposed of the garment, his voice a little thicker and slower than normal as he told her, 'Stop arguing, just for once. Any minute now you'll be out like a light. You might as well be comfortable.'

He dealt quickly and efficiently with the front fastening of her bra and slid the straps from her shoulders, his hands sliding silkily over her almost unbearably sensitised flesh. And Charley released her breath on a slow, extended sigh and felt every last vestige of nerve-racking tension leave her body, leaving her limply languorous, her eyes unquestionably dreamy as she glanced down at the pale twin globes crested with rosy, tumescent peaks, then across to his face.

He had hunkered down in front of her, and the black, hooded eyes drifted with tantalising slowness from peak to peak then lazily upwards to lock with hers. She could happily drown in those eyes, and she could see the tiny jerk of a muscle at the side of his jaw, and her lips parted with a knowing, gentle smile as she dropped dreamily back against the pillows.

How wonderful if he were to make love to her like this, when her brain was too fuddled by the tablets he had given her to put up any resistance. Her whole body had gone boneless, melting, waiting for his possession. She closed her eyes blissfully, felt him lift her legs up on to the bed, and made a tiny murmur of wanton anticipation deep in her throat. She felt like purring, holding up her arms to welcome his embrace, but discovered she was too tired to move a muscle.

She wanted to open her eyes when she felt the tug at the waistband of her skirt, but the lids were too heavy, and when he slid her briefs down the length of her legs she knew her brain was incapable of raising any of those former, tiresome objections and welcomed the knowledge, concentrating with every last scrap of her remaining consciousness on savouring fully what he was about to do to her, on the possessive slide of his body between her welcoming thighs, the hard weight of him pinning her to the mattress as he slowly, thrustingly, slaked his considerable passion within the moist sheath of her body.

And then she felt the cool shock of silken sheets against her warm flesh, the brush of his lips against her forehead, and experienced a moment of blind, icy panic before she slid into unconsciousness.

Someone was moving about the room, opening the louvres, admitting the morning sunlight. Teresa, or Pilar. One or the other.

Charley shifted comfortably in the sumptuous bed. She was naked beneath the silk covering. Frowning, groping for a memory that seemed tantalisingly beyond her grasp, she wondered how she had got to bed. She could remember having the mother and father of all headaches—all down to Sebastian, of course. But little else. Except—oh, of course—Teresa had brought her some pain-killers and warm milk.

She shuddered, remembering the taste. The tablets must have been pretty potent; she must have gone out like a light, crawling between the sheets, not bothering to tug her nightdress over her head.

Not to worry; whatever Teresa had given her had done the trick. She felt absolutely fine now, fully rested. She would get her packing done in no time at all; no need to dwell on the fact that she would be leaving, and that there was definitely no coming back this time. No point in allowing herself to get into a state over what was inevitable.

She pulled herself up against the pillows and went rigidly still as she heard him say, 'Awake at last? Good.'

Not Teresa or Pilar at all! Grabbing for the sheet, she tugged it up to her chin, keeping it firmly there. And her eyes went like saucers as he walked into her line of vision, collecting a fresh vase of the long-stemmed white roses she loved from the top of a tallboy.

'For you. I picked them at dawn.' He put the blooms on the bedside table, his eyes liquid. 'How are you? I looked in on you several times during the night. You slept like a baby.'

'I'm fine, thank you.' The thought of him watching her while she slept was unnerving. 'The roses are lovely.' A pity she wouldn't be here to enjoy them. She gave him a brittle smile and added pointedly, 'I'd like to get dressed now.'

'Right.' He had his hands on his lean hips, his feet planted apart, grinning down on her, looking amazingly boyish.

He could, or so it seemed, lop a good ten years off his age at will. When she reached the age of forty she would very likely envy him that ability. But by the time she was forty she would have forgotten his existence, or he would have become, at the very least, a dim and distant memory, she reminded herself. And if he thought she was going to get dressed while he was in the same room . . . She glowered at him, and he smiled right back at her and sat down on the edge of the bed.

'We'll spend the day in the mountains. You always enjoyed doing that.'

So she had. But mostly she had driven herself. He had only made time to take her once, and that during the very early days of their marriage, part of a honeymoon that had lasted precisely four days before he had immersed himself in his never-ending work. Her mouth went firm as she recalled how she would return from those trips, babbling on and on about what she had seen, where she had been, hoping against futile hope that her enthusiasm might induce him to spare her some of his precious time, repeat that solitary outing.

But she wasn't going to remind him of that. It wouldn't do to jog his memory, let him know she had cared too much. Instead, she pointed out, 'I'm going back to England today, if I'm in time to get a flight.'

He didn't seem too perturbed at having his much too tardy offer tossed back in his face. He simply tilted his head on one side and gave her the benefit of a long, warmly searching look.

'What's the mad hurry? You were prepared to spend four weeks here—you've got three and a half to go.'

True, but, crazy about him though she might be, she wasn't completely mad! She would never be able to hide her feelings if she spent that much time in his company.

'That was when I was anxious for our divorce to go through as quickly as possible,' she pointed out in a stiff little voice she hardly recognised as her own.

He acknowledged her point with a dip of his disgracefully handsome head and she watched him suspiciously, sure he was hiding a smug grin at her expense. But he was perfectly straight-faced when he met her wary golden eyes and told her, 'I accept that. Now that the putative second husband has left in what was probably a state of high dudgeon, you're quite free to go whenever you please. However...'

That look of bland innocence had never rung true, not even when she had, figuratively at least, been in the habit of lying on her back, waving her arms and legs in the air, waiting for her tummy to be tickled like the silly bitch she'd been, whenever he had appeared. And now it made her fingers tighten on the jade silk sheets, her eyes wide and wary. But when he continued, 'A couple of days' delay won't hurt you, surely? Look on it as a well earned holiday. I'm sure we're both adult enough to spend a little time together relaxing without flying at each other's throats,' she had to admit he was right.

Where was the harm? As long as she remembered that he had never really cared for her, of course, and kept the cold, hard truth of it well to the forefront of her mind as an insurance against her own weakness where he was concerned.

Besides, his earlier reference to Greg had made her wonder if a hasty departure was a sensible course to take. They might find themselves returning on the same flight, occupying adjacent seats. Oh, heaven forbid!

She would be running across him, inevitably, when she returned to her job. It was a small community and she couldn't hope to avoid him forever. She wasn't a moral coward—at least she hoped not—but he would never accept that their marriage could never have worked, and would always believe that she had treated him shabbily, hoping for a reconciliation with her estranged but wealthy husband for purely mercenary reasons.

And how he would gloat when her return to England demonstrated his scornful warning that Sebastian would throw her out, because what could such a man want with a woman like her? She would have to endure it, eventually—that and his sulks—but not before absolutely necessary.

'Agreed?'

The way his black eyes crinkled at the corners made him irresistible, but that had nothing to do with her decision, of course it hadn't. And just to show him she wasn't much bothered either way, she gave an uninterested shrug of her slender shoulders and told him coolly, 'Very well. Just a couple of days. And the mountains would be nice.'

And she refused to look at him, staring with apparent fascination at one of the bedposts, not moving a muscle until he levered himself off the edge of the bed and walked out of the room, telling her, 'I'll have the car waiting in twenty minutes.' A very fractional pause and then, his voice deepening, 'I promise to give you a day to remember.'

CHAPTER EIGHT

A DAY to remember. Charley refused to think about that. It didn't mean a thing. Sebastian had the unhappy knack of making a woman feel special. A word or a look was all it took to make any female he happened to be with, whatever her age or situation, feel as if she were the only woman in the world. And as soon as she was out of sight he forgot she existed, while she...

But she, Charley, had the benefit of experience. She knew better than to attach any significance to those melting looks or the words that tripped so easily from his honeyed tongue.

After a quick shower she dressed in a pair of well washed, well worn loose-fitting cotton trousers and topped them with a long-sleeved button-to-the-neck blouse. An adequate protection from the burning rays of the sun, not to mention Sebastian's burning eyes.

Satisfied that the way she looked offered no provocation whatsoever, she caught up her shady-brimmed straw hat and her bag and went slowly down the beautiful staircase, quietly confident that she would be able to make the most of the unexpected holiday and keep her reactions to her husband firmly under control. They might even be able to talk sensibly about the details of their coming divorce, like the mature adults they were meant to be.

Ignazia was on her hands and knees washing the vast marble floor, so it must be much earlier than she had supposed. Charley grinned down at the ancient woman as they exchanged greetings. She came from the hills and was as thin as a stick, but had enough energy for twenty. Ignazia had boasted that her mother had lived to be a hundred and two and that she fully intended to do better. Charley, for one, firmly believed she would achieve her objective without any trouble at all.

'Ignazia, you do know that machines can be bought which are capable of doing that job for you? You'd only have to press a switch—nothing to be frightened of, I promise.' Sebastian appeared in the vast doorway, sunlight streaming in from the courtyard behind him, the warmth of his smile encompassing Charley as she picked her way carefully over the wet floor.

'*Sí*, Don Sebastian, I do know.' Ignazia sat back on her heels, wringing her cloth over the bucket with steely wrists. 'I also know that no machine can do the work as well as I. When I am dead and buried you can buy your machine. And much happiness may it bring you!'

'Grief!'

Sebastian held out his hand to Charley, his black eyes dancing. And she took it without thinking, enjoying this moment of shared amusement, meeting his smile with one of her own as he muttered, 'I am surrounded by stubborn old women! What is a mere male to do?'

'You wouldn't have it any other way,' Charley chided him softly as they descended the steps to the courtyard together. The fierce pride and independence of these Gaditanos ran through every level of society; it was one of the things that made them unique, certainly something that he, for one, wouldn't

have any different. Which explained why he tolerated
Teresa's sharp tongue and definite ideas when a
foreigner in his position would have booted her out
for insubordination years ago!

'You are probably right,' he conceded, tucking her
hand in the crook of his arm. 'Teresa has packed us
a hamper, and I thought we'd set out early, before
the heat becomes too fierce. But if you'd like to have
breakfast first...?'

'No, let's get moving.'

The holiday mood had infected her; she would have
to take care not to lower her guard too much, she
cautioned herself as he saw her settled in the
comfortable passenger seat, taking herself firmly in
hand and merely nodding when he told her, with a
warmly flickering sideways glance, 'We'll stop at one
of the villages for coffee; have you any preference?'

'Not really. You choose. I'm in your hands.' Which
hadn't been a particularly sensible choice of words,
she grumbled to herself as she felt her cheeks flame
when she saw his lips twitch, one dark, strongly
marked brow arching upwards with hateful male
smugness.

But to put him straight, tell him forcefully that she
hadn't meant it literally, would only draw his attention to her agitation, and amuse him no end. So
she compressed her lips and stared straight ahead,
thankful that getting the big car through the narrow
streets and heading out of town took all his
concentration.

Once off the main roads and heading for the hills,
Charley relaxed. It was impossible not to. The narrow
road swooped upwards to the blue arc of the sky, and
below them, in the river valley, lay one of the first of

the white villages, approached, as almost always, by a fine old stone bridge.

'We'll try there,' Sebastian suggested, turning the car on to the descending track, and she was glad to agree, avidly picking out the details of the spire of the lofty church, the thread of cooking smoke from the breakfast *churros* in the air.

And then, the car neatly parked in the square, she had to stop herself forcibly from reaching for his hand as they wandered together towards a likely-looking café, their sauntering progress watched by a handful of old ladies smothered in shawls who stared unblinkingly from their doorways.

She loved the colourful vitality of this land. It brought a lump to her throat, a painful poignancy, because she knew she would never visit again. In a couple of days she would be returning to England, starting out all over again on the long and difficult road to self-sufficiency, learning to forget Sebastian.

Stoically, she swallowed the lump in her throat. Surely she deserved to allow herself to enjoy just this one day? There couldn't be any real harm in it, not if she kept her head and didn't allow her feelings for him to get a look-in.

'Happy?' he asked gently as he led her to one of the tables outside the café and saw her settled. Dressed in pale grey chinos and a loose black shirt, he looked spectacular. But then he always did, whatever he wore. It was nothing new.

Dragging in a long, steadying breath, she tore her eyes from his and gave him a brief nod. Yes, she was happy. For the moment. For as long as she forgot who he was, what he had meant to her, what he still

meant to her. As long as she concentrated on her surroundings, she was happy.

'Good.' The warmth of his eyes, the lilt of his lips,
told her he'd taken her admission at face value, never
guessing the restrictions she placed upon it. But that
wasn't important.

As he ordered coffee and *churros* she simply relaxed and soaked up the atmosphere, timeless in spite
of the odd truck or two, the ubiquitous motorbikes,
with the cobbled streets fanning out from the square
with its crumbling architecture, the stone fountain
surrounded by chattering women in the centre. And
flowers everywhere—in urns, in billowing gardens,
hanging from balconies, in patios glimpsed through
the grilled doors of the larger houses. And the grocer's
shop with its hanging hams and garlic and sausages.
And old men playing dominoes in the dim recesses of
the café behind them . . .

'Shall we move on?' His quiet voice was in tune
with her mood. They hadn't exchanged above half a
dozen words as they had breakfasted on strong black
café solo and *churros*—rings of batter fried in
smoking hot oil and coated with sugar—but the silence
had been comfortable.

Licking the last grains of sugar from her fingers,
she stood up and waited while he paid the bill, and
as they strolled back towards the car he slipped an
arm around her waist and drew her close to his side
and she didn't object, simply allowed it to happen.

Pushing him away, telling him to keep his hands to
himself, would strike a sour, contentious note. She
didn't want that. Not today. She wanted today to be
perfect, a thing apart, picked out from the thousands
of flawed hours they had spent together. Something

to remember with affection and gratitude down through the years.

And she was glad she had made no objections when they headed deeper into the hills. The atmosphere in the car was mellow, curling around them both, drawing them together with a gentle, lazy insistence that was difficult to deny. And her state of happiness was a thing of vibrant flamboyance, beating wildly inside her as they left the car at the end of a stony track and, carrying the hamper between them, ambled slowly onwards and upwards to where the stone crags met the brazen blue sky and kites hovered on the thermals, watching them.

Then down by unspoken consent, down towards a hollow of verdant green on the banks of a bubbling trout stream. Sebastian took her end of the hamper, standing aside to let her scramble down the narrow track, following sure-footedly despite his burden.

'Here, I think.' He put the hamper down in the shade of a cork oak, a stone's throw from the stream, and Charley flopped cross-legged on to the springy grass, flapping her hat in front of her face to create a breeze. 'Wine?' he asked, and she nodded, not looking at him, because he was too sensational. He hurt her heart.

But that was idiotic. The whole point of today was simply to relax and enjoy, and that meant not allowing him to affect her, refusing to allow herself to remember . . .

Teresa had done them proud. There were two bottles of white wine, which Sebastian immediately took down to the cold waters of the mountain stream to cool, leaving her to rummage among the other goodies: wedges of cold *tortilla á la española*, the thick golden egg and potato cake, chunks of home-made bread wrapped up in white linen napkins, covered bowls of several different delicious salads, luscious fresh fruit, olives and crystal glasses ...

'Now I know why the hamper weighed a ton!' She grinned up at him as he loomed above her. But the sparkle left her eyes; she felt it go, knew she must look wary now. More than wary. Because he looked dangerous and piratical, a lock of black hair tumbling over his forehead, hands on his hips, his bare feet planted apart, the bottoms of his trousers rolled up to just below his knees, droplets of stream water glistening against his skin.

Damn! Her entire body was responding to his potent sexuality, her breasts peaking, fire licking her thighs. Oh, damn it! Why did it have to be like this?

Concentrate on the food, on eating, she instructed herself. He was on the grass beside her, thankfully oblivious of the way she felt, forking selections of good things on to two china plates.

But no, the narrow-eyed look of frank and slow assessment he gave her when she took the plate he offered with a hand that shook disgracefully told her he wasn't oblivious at all. But, to give him his due, he didn't attempt to capitalise on her weakness, simply watched from lazily hooded eyes, which meant, of course, that she couldn't eat a thing.

'I rather think we might be ready for the wine, don't you?' Not waiting for an answer, he loped back to the stream and returned with one of the bottles. 'The water's icy, so it should be cool enough now.'

The words were prosaic enough, as were his actions with the corkscrew. But there was nothing prosaic at all about the soft sensuality of his voice, the way he looked at her. It made her heart leap wildly beneath her breastbone, as out of control as her pulses.

Her mouth was drier than a desert, and she took the glass he held out to her and drained half the contents in one gulp.

'You needed that.' His smile told her he knew exactly how she felt, the slow, lazy burn deep in his eyes conveying the information that he was content to wait for what he no doubt deemed the inevitable. Sebastian was no callow youth with no finesse and even less control. Not for him a quick tumble on the grass...

So it was up to her to let him know he was mistaken, wasn't it? That nothing was inevitable...

Charley drank the rest of the wine and held out the glass to him, saying with quiet defiance, 'I was thirsty, yes. Perhaps I'll be able to eat something now.'

An olive. Just a single olive. Her throat closed up at the mere thought of trying to swallow anything else. It was shaming. She couldn't have better told him the way he made her feel if she'd shouted it from the hilltop.

She was actually quivering, and hated herself for reacting to him this way, and she fully expected him to make some comment on her obvious state of aroused awareness, but all he did was refill her glass then lie back on the sun-warmed grass, his arms folded behind his head.

Which gave her some breathing space.

But she couldn't bear to look at him. The temptation to stretch out beside him, to wriggle close to him and await the delicious consequences, was far too great. Self-control was needed, as never before. She really shouldn't have agreed to come.

Sensibly, she turned her back on him and, not so sensibly, sipped at her refill until the glass was empty and her head was beginning to spin. Risking a glance over her shoulder, she put the glass down near the hamper. He seemed to be asleep, dark lashes soft, relaxed crescents, his wide chest slowly rising and falling.

The moments of very real danger had obviously passed. He had known how he affected her, been fully aware that he had only needed to touch her to set her on fire with a desire that couldn't be contained, yet he hadn't bothered. It hadn't been worth the effort.

And that was a relief, wasn't it? Yes, most certainly it was! And her heart wasn't twisting with pain. Of course it wasn't. It was just the effects of two glasses of wine, taken too quickly. And the sun was burning down, and with a whimper she didn't even try to explain away to herself she shifted further into the shade of the cork oak, swallowed the ridiculous lump in her throat, and curled up against the grass, making herself relax.

Gradually, the sweet silence and emptiness of the landscape, the warm, aromatic scent of rosemary, thyme and lavender combined with the unbelievable headiness of a million wild flowers, began to soothe the ambivalence of her emotions, helping her to make some sense of them. Yes, she wanted Sebastian's lovemaking until the need was a physical pain inside her. But she wanted more, so much more. Wanted his love. And he couldn't give her that. Which left her with nothing.

No, not nothing, she corrected herself drowsily. It left her with safety.

Being safe from the pain he could dole out was all she needed, she consoled herself, slipping over the edge into sleep, recalling just fleetingly as she dropped the way he had undressed her last night, the way she had felt. She had forgotten the incident, or blocked it out of her mind. But she was glad it had surfaced now. It would help her hide her feelings more securely in the little time they had left together, and it meant that the danger from him wasn't too great.

He could have made love to her all night. No problem. She had been more than willing. He must have had some inkling, surely? He was a very experienced male animal. But he hadn't bothered. He had always been able to take her or leave her. Where she was concerned his emotions had never been involved...

And her last thought, before sleep finally claimed her, was that she had a lot to be thankful for. It would have been too humiliating for words if he had realised just how very much she had wanted him to make love to her. How she had actually expected it to happen. And maybe, just maybe, he had merely thought that she'd zonked out, drugged to the eyeballs by whatever was in those potent painkillers. She took what comfort she could from that...

Idly, she brushed the insect away from the curve of her cheek. It didn't budge, simple renewed its aggravating, feather-light attack. She grumbled sleepily and turned on her side, burrowing the exposed skin of her face into her arms.

Tenaciously, the wretched thing walked over the nape of her neck. A skin covered with unsightly red bumps would be all she would have to show for her stay in Spain, she thought irritably, hauling herself back to full consciousness, twisting on to her back again and opening her eyes to find Sebastian sitting on the ground beside her, his knees drawn up to his chin, a long feathery grass dangling between his fingers.

'Oh, how hilarious!' she said with grumpy sarcasm, hating the way her stomach jolted inside her at waking to find herself the object of his amused attentions. But he just smiled at her, that slow, knowing smile that sent her pulses haywire and made her breath come in little jerks, making her breasts rise and fall too rapidly, pushing against the thin cotton of her blouse.

And he just watched her as she scrambled up to her feet and brushed stray pieces of dried grass from her crumpled trousers, his half-hooded eyes never leaving her face. And she glared right back at him; he was making her very uneasy. He was good at that; he didn't even have to think about it. He just did it.

She dragged her eyes away and swivelled round, and he asked, his voice hoarse and sexy, 'Where are you going?'

'To cool off.' To give herself a little breathing space. To wake up properly. To clear her head and find the ability to pretend. Pretend she was in control of the situation. Pretend they were simply two acquaintances who were enjoying a break together.

On the banks of the stream she removed her canvas shoes and rolled up her trousers and stepped into the water. It swirled around her calves and was icy-cold. Just what she needed. And she waded a little way downstream, taking care because the flat rocks were slippery beneath her feet, and then froze, her stomach jolting, when his dark voice came from right behind her.

'Be careful. The rocks can be treacherous.'

Charley turned very slowly, forcing herself to face him. She hadn't expected him to follow her, but she could handle it. It needn't be a problem.

He towered above her, of course, and the breadth of his shoulders cut out the sun. And he was grinning, his teeth very white against the tanned olive skin. A warm breeze winnowed softly over the hillside, coming from the south. It lifted the silky soft black strands of his hair, and she had an overpowering urge to run her fingers through it, to revel in the vital texture, touch the warm, hard bones of his skull.

Oh, God, will it never end? she thought wildly as the intense pain of loving him cut through her, making her bite down hard on her soft lower lip, stepping back from him abruptly, her feet sliding from under her on the slippery surface of a submerged rock. And she screeched with shock as she sat down in a great whoosh of spray, the icy water up to her waist.

Trust her! she derided, mortified, taking no comfort from his obvious concern as he took her hands in his and gently hauled her to her feet.

'Have you hurt yourself?'

He lifted her by the elbows and set her on the bank, and she denied, pouting, 'No.' Only her dignity. At the moment she felt numb from the waist down, but that was only the effect of the cold mountain water. Tomorrow she would be covered in bruises and might need to take a cushion wherever she went. But for now, 'No,' she repeated, pushing at his hands. 'You can let go of me. I don't intend to give an encore.'

'I'm glad to hear it. A repeat performance wouldn't be nearly as amusing.' His black eyes crinkled at her, and her own mouth twitched in unwilling response, and he said, putting her right back on her guard,

'You'd better take those trousers off. Spread them out in the sun; they'll be dry in no time.'

'I'd rather not.' She sounded prim, she knew she did, but what did that matter? No way was she going to prance around in front of him wearing a lacy pair of really rather skimpy briefs.

It wasn't that she didn't trust him. He'd had his chance last night and hadn't taken it, which meant that either he wasn't interested or he wasn't as astute at reading her feelings as she'd imagined. No, it was herself she didn't trust.

But she couldn't tell him that. Couldn't tell him that if she got herself all wound up she could end up making him an offer he might stir himself to accept— despite the fact that he'd already taken his planned revenge and ruined her relationship with Greg.

And then where would she be? More besotted than ever, the pain of parting, of the coming divorce, doubly intolerable.

'Don't be pigheaded, Charlotte. There's no one to see you.' His fingers were at the waistband of her sodden trousers, the backs curled against the suddenly quivering flesh of her stomach as he untucked the dripping tails of her blouse.

'There's you,' she pointed out, her voice mortifyingly unsteady, but he merely smiled the slow, secretive smile that turned her bones to water and her brains to mush, and began, methodically, to unbutton her blouse, and told her,

'I've seen you in much less; last night—remember?—to mention the most recent occasion.' The buttons parted from their anchorage. He slipped his hands beneath the cotton and cupped the smooth curve of her shoulders. 'You can't deny I behaved perfectly. I didn't touch—well, not as much as I would have liked to. I will admit I looked.' He slipped the blouse down her arms and let it drop to the ground, his eyes dropping too, to the pouting globes of her breasts, the taut peaks only too clearly visible through the fragile covering of lace.

He was mesmerising her. The touch of his eyes as they grazed her swollen, inviting breasts was sending her wild, everything inside her going haywire, in spite of all her good intentions.

And at last, at long last, those dark eyes lifted to her mouth and she caught the brilliant glitter beneath the heavy lids, and her lips parted on a gasp of submission that was as old as Eve and the glitter intensified, just briefly, before he dipped his head and slowly, oh, so erotically, circled her lips with his tongue, moistening them for her, before he bent to suckle her through the straining lace, and she heard him mutter thickly, heard him above the incredible pounding of her blood, 'I am your husband, Charlotte. Entitled to touch as well as look.'

Oh, God! she cried in silent anguish as the pleasure-pain of what he was doing to her intensified until she almost sobbed aloud with the glory of it. Why did he have to remind her?

Legally, he was still her husband, but not in any real sense. Could it be that his need for revenge was still unsatisfied, that he meant to enslave her all over again before cutting her out of his life? Could he be that arrogant, that cruel?

But her fingers were frantically twining in the thick darkness of his hair, as if they had a mind of their own, her head flung back on the arching column of her slender neck, and all she could manage was a dis-gracefully husky reminder, 'We're getting divorced.'

'Who said so?' He didn't even lift his head. He was shaking all over as he dropped to his knees and dragged her sodden garments down from her hips. And she knew his control was going as he rested the hard angle of his cheek against the dark curls that covered her sex, a fierce possessive pride in his voice as he demanded, 'Stay. Be my wife again, Charlotte.'

Stay? She went very still, every sense on red alert. It would be too easy to agree. Far, far too easy. But she would never put herself through that again. Never.

Going for weeks, hardly seeing him at all. Just the occasional late supper together. Lying alone in that great big bed, wondering if he would come to her. Pathetically eager when he did, pining and anxious through all those long, lonely nights when he didn't. Knowing he didn't love her, distressingly aware that her love for him had made her a slave. A doormat.

'No!' Gathering strength from somewhere, she pushed him away. 'And please don't touch me! I won't stay and go through all——'

'*Bastante!*' He had gone beyond listening to anything she might have to say. He caught her round her knees and tumbled her to the grass, his big body pinning her to the ground, one of his knees wrenching her thighs apart, his mouth cruel as he dragged his shirt off in one violent, ripping movement. 'You drive me wild and then say "Don't touch"! Do you want me to lose my reason?'

'No.' Her breath was coming in ragged gasps, but she met the wild blackness of his eyes bravely, begging him, 'Don't do this, Sebastian. Please don't do this.'

'Do what?' His mouth curled in bitter contempt. 'Make love to my wife?'

But it wasn't love. Just rampaging lust. He was aroused beyond control, and she had never seen him like this before. He had always been so much in command of every situation, of all his emotions. She couldn't bear to see him like this, as if he were being subjected to some kind of excruciating torture.

She had left him unsatisfied on the afternoon when she had left him to go and find Greg. And now she was doing it again. There was only so much a virile male could take. And it was as much her fault as his, she thought bleakly as she watched the battle going on in his fiery eyes.

She shouldn't have let him touch her, allowed his power over her senses to take control away from her mind. And all she wanted to do now was comfort him, wrap her arms around him and tell him she loved him, that there would never be, could never be, another man for her. She had gone down that road and it had led to a dead end.

But she didn't dare. She couldn't. She couldn't put herself through all that again. Not even for love of him. She would despise herself for the rest of her life if she did.

And she recognised the precise moment when the battle was won. If this cold, empty nothingness could be called winning.

His mouth compressed, his eyes mirroring his moment of deep self-contempt, before he moved away from her, reaching for his torn shirt and dragging it over his shoulders as he said in a cold, hard voice that made her shake inside, 'I'll ask one more time. Are you willing to put the misunderstandings of the past aside and stay with me? As my wife? Think about it, for a moment.'

She didn't need to be told that he would never ask her again. It was there in every tautly held muscle of his proud masculine body as he moved away to repack the hamper, giving her time. And when the last strap was buckled he picked up her scattered clothing, coming to her, helping her to her feet, into the damp garments, his hands surprisingly gentle.

But he didn't look directly at her. Not once. And when he said, his voice tight, 'Well? Do I have an answer?' her heart lurched sickeningly and she wondered, just wondered...Olivia was out of the equation now. Maybe he still missed the woman who had so obsessed him, mourned her in the dark, secret core of his heart. But Olivia had earned her banishment by lying as she had. Olivia would never have a place in Sebastian Machado's life again. Which left the other thing...

'You want children?' It came out sounding flat, already defeated. But she had to know. If he felt he needed her for other reasons, rather than simply that of getting an heir, then there might be, somehow, a chance for them...

For a moment there was a flicker of something entirely unreadable in the dark, burning intensity of the eyes that at last locked with hers. And then it was gone, leaving them flat and black, and his voice was unkind as he gave her the answer she had expected deep in her heart.

'What else?'

She turned away, desperately fighting tears then said simply, with a strange dignity that surprised her, 'I'm sorry.' More sorry than he would ever know. 'But the answer's still no.'

And he returned, with a stiff, prideful courtesy that made her blood run cold, 'As you wish, *señora*. As you wish.'

CHAPTER NINE

'No, I haven't a thing for you,' Freda stated decisively, drumming her fingers against the polished top of the desk. 'And I won't have for at least another two weeks.'

Charley leaned back in the high-backed wooden chair across the desk from her aunt's padded swivelling thing and met the cool grey eyes with a very slight sigh.

'What's this all about, Freda? You're always complaining you haven't enough first-class temps to satisfy all your would-be clients. Are the customers all deserting you in droves?'

If they were, then she would have to register with another agency, just for the time being, until things looked up again, but it didn't seem likely. Freda's agency was highly successful.

But Charley needed her work like a junkie needed a fix, and she tilted one eyebrow across the desk space, waiting for some kind of explanation.

The years hadn't softened Freda. There was no warmth in the severe cast of her features, framed as they were by that austerely sculpted iron-grey hair, but there was a note of rough, almost grudging affection in the other woman's voice when she stated, 'You need a holiday. That's what this is all about. You haven't had a break since you joined me in June. Which wouldn't be anything to make a song and dance about in normal circumstances, I grant you.' She pressed the buzzer of the intercom on her desk and demanded a tray of tea.

'But have you looked at yourself recently? You look like death.'

'Oh, what rubbish!' Charley unclenched her hands and clasped them lightly together on her lap, forcing herself to relax. 'I'm as fit as a fiddle. Besides, hard work never hurt anyone.'

Hard work was all she had—that and her long-term plan for survival.

'I'll agree with you on that.' Freda permitted herself a very small smile. 'After all, I'm living testimony. However...' She dipped her head in acknowledgment as Ruth, her secretary, walked in with the requested tea-tray, waiting until she left before continuing, 'But then I don't tie myself in painful emotional knots over a man. I've got more sense and more respect for my mental energies. Pour, would you, please?'

'You've got a nerve!' Charley spoke lightly, but she was seething inside as she got up to pour the tea. What did Freda know about emotional knots? She had never loved anyone or anything in her life, apart from the agency she'd built up from scratch.

'At my age I'm entitled to speak my mind.'

Was that a glint of humour in the steel-grey eyes? Charley couldn't be absolutely sure, but she handed her aunt the delicate china cup and saucer more graciously than she had previously felt inclined to.

'And to my mind you're heading for some kind of physical breakdown.' The grey eyes followed her niece as she took her own cup and resumed her seat. And as Charley opened her mouth to pour scorn on that opinion she overrode her strongly, 'If we are to stick to our original plans, then I need you strong and healthy, not coming down with every bug and virus going the rounds this winter. The cottage is empty now, and two weeks of fresh air with nothing to do but relax and build yourself up with good wholesome food should help, don't you think? You look as if you haven't eaten a square meal in months. You can take my car. I can manage perfectly well with taxis.'

Two weeks without work to occupy her mind would be hell. She wouldn't go. And she pointed out tartly, 'A fortnight without any earnings is not what I need, thanks all the same. You know how hard I'm saving.'

'Then you'll have to agree that a few months off because of ill health during this coming winter—flu, colds, sheer exhaustion—won't help your bank balance either,' Freda came back with horrible logic. 'Besides, it's not as if either one of us wants or expects you to buy into partnership with me tomorrow. It will take time for you to learn all the ropes. At the moment you're getting to know how to deal with our regular clients—and you haven't been thrown into the lion's den with the more ogrish of them yet, my dear! Then, of course, there will be the administration side of it. Quite a headache, I assure you. Do I have to go on?'

Not really.

As soon as she had returned from Spain she had handed her notice to Dev. It hadn't been because she'd felt unable to face Greg; she wasn't that much of a coward. But she'd needed a bigger challenge, to earn more than she could at the complex. Her future might stretch emptily in front of her, but she might as well make it as comfortable as possible, and as challenging.

Asking Freda for help hadn't been easy. She had never approved of her marriage to Sebastian and had made no bones about saying as much. She had been supportive when the marriage had broken up, making sure she finished her training, putting her forward for the job at the complex. But she had been coldly, incredulously angry when she'd learned that Charley planned to ask Sebastian for a divorce in person.

But Charley had swallowed her pride. What was the point of having an aunt who was in a position to help and not asking if she would put her on her books, arrange temping jobs for her?

And so, when her notice had been worked out, Charley, at her aunt's invitation, had spent a few days with her, staying at her flat in Harrow, to discuss the possibilities. And Freda had agreed that yes, she could help, that the remuneration from temping was excellent. But why didn't Charley consider saving hard and, after she'd learned the business from top to bottom, buying a full partnership in the firm?

It had seemed like a good idea. It still did. And she was saving every penny she could towards her future, against the day she would need to take out a bank loan to buy into the business.

'Well?' Freda looked pointedly at her watch.

Charley heaved a sigh and faced up to the immediate problem. If her aunt had decided she needed a holiday, then there would be no changing her mind. Whatever happened, she couldn't expect to be working for the next two weeks. She shrugged, accepting it as a fact of life, but not having to like it.

'If you insist I take time off, I will. But I don't fancy going to the cottage. Not at this time of the year. I'll probably redecorate the bed-sit.' Said to annoy. Which it did.

'Then you're more of a fool than I took you for!' Freda stood up, terminating the interview. 'The weather can be lovely on the Welsh coast in October, and the cottage is centrally heated, as you know. But if you'd rather grub around in that horrid little place of yours...' She dragged open a drawer in one of the filing-cabinets. 'If you change your mind, let me know and I'll give you the keys. Take the tray with you on your way out.'

Getting used to driving her aunt's car wasn't a problem; she had used it to pick up and deliver Freda's weekend groceries from time to time. And finding her way to the tiny Welsh coastal village was no hassle because she'd got an excellent road map on the passenger seat beside her.

The real problem was how to endure the empty two weeks ahead, how to deal with the lack of mental occupation without her aching regret over Sebastian flooding in to fill her head and mangle her heart.

Her original decision to redecorate the bed-sit— reached on an impulse as a way to let Freda know she couldn't dictate to her—had been a non-starter. It was, as her aunt had pointed out, a horrible little place. No amount of redecorating could make it any better.

It wasn't a home, just a place to sleep. There was barely room to move. But she had taken it because it had been cheap, letting her save more of her income, adding to what remained of her parents' legacy, which hadn't been large to start with, the outstanding mortgage and solicitor's bills swallowing up the bulk of it. And because she had balked at the idea of taking up Freda's offer of the more or less permanent use of the spare room at her flat. She did need some independence. But two weeks holed up there, on her own, dabbing paint around simply to let her aunt know she did have some freedom of choice, had seemed, in the end, pretty stupid.

So she was going to have to rusticate and make the best of it. And perhaps her aunt was right; perhaps loads of fresh air would help her sleep. She hadn't been sleeping properly, or eating, she admitted, since she'd left Cadiz on the day following that fateful picnic in the hills.

But how much fresh air and exercise would it take to stop those haunting dreams? Every night she relived their final confrontation, his stiff, ungiving silence as he'd driven her back to Cadiz.

And when she'd finally swallowed the pride that had forced her to hide her feelings from him because she couldn't take any more humiliation, and plucked up the courage to explain her refusal, to tell him she needed the love he was unable to give her, he hadn't wanted to listen, blocking off her first halting words with a stiff, unyielding, 'Don't waste your breath. There's nothing more to be said. It is all over.'

They were the last words he had ever spoken to her, yet she would hear them in her dreams, night after endless night. He had left her at the house, no explanations, and by the time she'd left for the airport on the morning of the following day he had still not returned.

The customary lump that clogged her throat whenever she was unguarded enough to think of him made her swallow in fierce self-disgust. She had to get over him, forget him. She had to! She couldn't wallow in misery for the rest of her life.

Besides, it was a beautiful autumn day, the sky crisp and blue, the trees already beginning to turn colour. And she had always loved the sea. She hadn't seen Freda's cottage before, but she'd seen photographs. Her aunt had bought it a few years ago for a future retirement home, letting it out during the summer months to hand-picked tenants, visiting it occasionally herself for a few days at a time.

Charley found it easily enough from Freda's detailed instructions. Approached by a narrow stone bridge, dripping with ivy, the cottage lay at the end of a track, surrounded by woodland at the head of the narrow valley that ran down to the coast.

The sea-front and village were a twenty-minute walk away, Freda had told her. There was a shop where she could buy fresh food, and the Evanses, whose farmhouse abutted the road opposite the bridge and the turn-off for the cottage, would sell her all the fresh eggs and milk she needed. And if anything went wrong—blocked drains, problems with the electricity supply, anything at all—she was to contact them. They were a very obliging family.

How obliging, she discovered as she parked her aunt's car in front of the cottage at the side of a battered Land Rover. It seemed odd that there should be anyone around; it was such an end-of-the-world sort of place, and there was a slight frown between her eyes as she slid out of the car and closed the door behind her. Walking round to the rear to open the boot and heave out her case, she heard the cottage door open and a woman's cheerful voice call out, 'Gwilym will do that for you. It's Charley, isn't it?' She bustled down the path, a short round woman wearing a faded, flower-print overall on top of a skirt and jumper. 'Your aunty phoned this morning to let us know you were coming. I've brought up eggs and milk and some of our own home-cured bacon, and turned on the immersion and central heating, ready. And Gwilym, my eldest, put a load of logs in the shed—the nights get chilly and an open fire's more company, isn't it?'

Charley assimilated the barrage of information, her smile growing wider by the moment, and when she took the woman's proffered hand she said, 'You must be Mrs Evans.'

'We don't stand on ceremony round here. Call me Peggy. Now where's that boy of mine got to?'

On cue, a youth strode along the flagged path that led to the back of the squat, stone-built cottage. He would be about eighteen, Charley guessed, not tall but stockily built, with friendly blue eyes in an attractive, nut-brown face and short, crinkly brown hair. He carried her case and the carton of essentials she'd brought with her—just tea and coffee and a selection of tinned foods—into the cottage, and Charley locked the car and followed, Peggy, chattering nineteen to the dozen, bringing up the rear.

Gwilym was promptly despatched upstairs to take the case, and Peggy led the way to the kitchen, where she filled the electric kettle for tea, told Charley where to find everything, and began to unpack the carton of provisions.

'You won't get far on this lot,' she remarked, putting away the few tins in one of the cupboards. 'Your aunty said you needed feeding up and I can see she was right. That's the trouble with girls today—they don't think they look right unless they're a bag of bones! I should have brought up one of my fruit cakes. Tell you what, why don't you have supper with us? We're having steak and kidney pudding with apple crumble for afters. Gwilym could come for you at around seven and bring you back later. You can manage that, can't you, Gwilym? You weren't planning on going out later? Mind you, even if you were, Dai—he's my husband,' she explained to Charley, 'would see you home safely. It's a law-abiding part of the world, but you can never be too sure, can you? And I promised your aunty I'd keep an eye on you.'

'I'd be pleased to,' Gwilym affirmed shyly, when he could get a word in.

He was hovering in the open kitchen doorway, and Charley, putting the cups and saucers out on the kitchen table, said firmly, 'It's a kind offer, Peggy, but I'll be spending the evening settling in and getting my bearings. And I'll probably have an early night.' She reached the jug of milk from the fridge and poured the tea. 'Now how much do I owe you for the food and logs?'

Already she was feeling swamped, the small kitchen made claustrophobic by Peggy's endless chatter and Gwilym's hovering silence, the way he watched her every movement with those crinkling, twinkling eyes.

'Nothing,' Peggy dismissed the offer of payment, sitting down to her cup of tea. 'I've got an arrangement with your aunty. Gwilym and I see to the place—he looks after the garden and outside stuff and I keep the inside tidy. I clean up when her holiday tenants leave, see the electricity's off, turn off the water and drain the pipes before winter sets in. She settles up at the end of each month and she made a point of asking me to see you supplied with things to tempt your appetite.' She stirred her tea furiously, as if regretting the lack of sugar. 'I do wish I'd thought to bring that fruit cake. We could have had a slice with our tea; it would have gone down a treat.'

Any moment now, the obliging Gwilym would be sent rattling down the track in the Land Rover to fetch the regretted cake. Charley couldn't bear it.

'It would have been waste of time as far as I'm concerned. I don't have a sweet tooth.' And she drained her cup and took it over to the sink, wondering if her dismissive action was too pointed.

Peggy meant well, but smothering was something Charley could do without. She was perfectly capable of looking after herself; how could Freda have suggested she wasn't? She must know what Peggy was like; did it amuse her to think of her niece being hounded by fruit cakes and farmhouse suppers, and strenuous, well meaning efforts to turn a 'bag of bones' into a billowy sack of undiluted cholesterol?

Charley put a match to the kindling and straightened up to close the curtains against the wet and windy darkness outside. She'd been at the cottage for a week now, and today had brought the first break in the lovely autumnal weather. Which meant she hadn't been able to wander the woods, stroll on the deserted beach or explore the coastal path. So she'd driven to the county town, spent the morning in and out of shops, browsing, and the afternoon in the company of a few snuffling senior citizens watching a film she'd had no real interest in seeing. The place had reeked of damp overcoats and peppermints, and she'd regretted the boredom that had sent her inside.

So if it carried on like this—which Gwilym, arriving on the doorstep this morning with the daily offering of foodstuffs from his mum, had gloomily predicted it would—she would pack her bags and head back to the despised bed-sit, and hound Freda, day and night if necessary, until she gave her another working assignment.

She had done her bit, taken a holiday, and she had even forced herself to eat properly. But the extra pounds she might have gained had been exercised off in her need to tire herself out so that she could sleep at night.

Surely Freda wouldn't expect her to stay on in weather like this, cooped up alone with nothing at all to occupy her mind? And she really couldn't accept all the invitations that came from the Evanses. She didn't want company. The only companion she needed was . . . Quickly she blanked out that train of thought and sat down, cross-legged, on the hearth rug, her hands clasped round her jeans-clad knees, staring into the flames, listening to the rain lashing against the windows.

And something else, something that wasn't the rain or the wind. A vehicle approaching up the track.

Sighing, Charley wriggled to her feet and tugged the apricot-coloured sweatshirt she was wearing down over her hips. Gwilym. Who else would be driving up the dead-end track at nine o'clock on a wild wet evening? He couldn't be bringing more offerings of food or milk, surely? She'd told him this morning that her fridge was overflowing!

She hoped he hadn't come to renew this morning's offer to take her to the village hop. It was, apparently, a monthly event and was set for tomorrow evening. And she'd told him that if the weather stayed wet she wouldn't be here, balking at an outright rejection, because she knew he only meant to be kind. He probably felt sorry for her because she was alone, and she couldn't stand that. Besides, she would be poor company.

Groaning as she heard the clunk of a vehicle door directly outside, she went to the main door which opened into the sitting-room, the staircase running up behind, and tugged it open, trying to smile, trying not to look as irritable as she felt. Then she gasped, her body going very cold as she encountered Sebastian's bleak black eyes.

He was the very last person she had expected to see and her shock must have registered, because he told her, the cold formality of his beautiful voice making her heart twist with pain, 'I would have let you know I was on my way, but your aunt assured me the cottage had no phone.'

Freda? Surely she hadn't told him she was here, given directions? But she must have done. Why, when she had so heartily disapproved of her relationship with Sebastian Machado right from the beginning?

And she'd been appalled by the state her niece had been in when she'd returned from Spain in May with her plans to marry the sound and suitable Greg completely abandoned, telling her roundly that the sooner she forgot the existence of 'that man', the better for the peace of mind of all concerned.

'May I come in?' His cold voice reminded her of the drenching rain, of the way she was hanging on to the door as if it were a lifeline. Expelling a shaky breath, she stepped aside, despising herself for the way her stomach lurched in unstoppable response as he brushed past her.

She had no idea why he had come. He had told her with cutting directness that everything was over between them. It was probably something to do with the divorce, she told herself as she closed the door on the wind and rain. Something that could be best discussed in person.

She was not going to allow herself to hope that it could be anything else, that he had actually wanted to see her. Nevertheless, her heart was beating like a crazy thing as she turned back into the body of the room, her legs shaky, barely able to support her weight.

His black hair, the shoulders of his elegantly cut dark blue business suit, were shimmering with drops of rain-water, and he turned from his brief contemplation of the fire, straddling the hearth, watching her as she edged round to the back of one of the armchairs, unthinkingly putting it between them, a barrier of sorts against the awful, coldly implacable uninterest of his presence.

And his black eyes said nothing to her. They looked as if they had watched a million years go by and could no longer find anything to interest them. Her throat tightened. All that shattering charm had gone, leaving no trace of the wicked smile, the gleam in the eyes that had promised heaven, not a single trace of the man he had been.

'You needn't hide. I'm not going to leap on you. That wasn't why I came.'

Slow colour stained her face as he made her aware of what she had done. Unconscious body language had a lot to answer for, she mourned, fighting embarrassment. And there was nothing she could say to excuse her defensive actions, so she rested her arms on the back of the chair and asked, echoing his coldness, 'Why did you come?'

A wintry smile touched his lips. 'To make you a business offer, what else? Your aunt wrote to me a short time ago—but you'll know all about that, of course.' The line of his mouth went bitter. 'Couldn't you bring yourself to contact me directly? Did you have to use her as a go-between?'

'Freda?' Charley's eyes were dark with bewilderment. What in the name of sweet reason was he talking about? Why on earth would Freda have written to him? She could barely bring herself to mention his name!

'How many aunts have you got?' He sounded utterly bored, turning back to the fire and holding his hands out to the flames. 'You appear to be very comfortable here. From Freda's letter I gathered you rarely stopped working to breathe. However——' he turned back to face her '—we can discuss that later.'

Again, the wintry smile. 'Do you think your charming welcome could extend as far as the offer of coffee?'

Did he have to be quite so sarcastic? Charley fumed, a spurt of temper making her eyes glitter like shards of amber glass. She drew herself stiffly upright, dragging her breath in through pinched nostrils, glaring at him suspiciously as the black eyes gleamed for a brief heartbeat of time, an unnerving echo of the Sebastian of old, as he commented, 'I see I'm still able to make you lose your temper.' Then the gleam was gone, and perhaps she had just imagined it, because the heavily lidded eyes were completely without expression, his voice as coldly, formally polite as ever as he explained, 'It's been a long drive, and the car I hired at Gatwick this morning has a malfunctioning heater. I'm cold.'

And tired, and hungry, Charley added in her head, reading the lines of strain on the hard-bitten features. If he'd driven from Gatwick to Harrow and then straight on here, then he must be all three.

Ignoring the quick pang of compassion, she made her face expressionless and went to put more logs on the fire, dusting her hands off as he sank down into one of the armchairs, his long legs outstretched.

'Of course,' she answered his request. 'And something to eat? An omelette?' One way of using up some of all those eggs, she thought, deliberately keeping her mind on the prosaic, carefully not looking at him. It hurt too much. Fool that she was, she couldn't stop loving him. She was afraid it would show in her eyes.

And she was out of the room and into the kitchen at a trot, not waiting for his answer, closing the door behind her and sagging against it, the palms of her hands splayed out on the cool wood.

It had been months since she'd seen him last, and the longing hadn't abated. Her struggle to come to terms with the end of their marriage was even worse than it had been four years ago. Much worse. And, heaven knew, it had been difficult enough then, even with the smoke-screen of Olivia's lies to cling on to.

And oh, how tenaciously she had clung to it, hidden behind it. Sebastian had killed his own brother; the police had suspected it and Olivia had known it. No one could love a cold-blooded killer; therefore it followed that she didn't. Or so she had convinced herself.

She could have no more admitted the truth—that she had left him because he hadn't loved her. He had loved Olivia, and she, Charley, was dispensable, would be tossed aside as soon as she had served her purpose. She hadn't been mature enough to tell him.

Was she mature enough now? Did she perhaps need to put everything straight, completing the circle? If the whole truth were told, the loose ends tied up, maybe she would be able, finally, to put the past behind her.

Biting down on her lip, she pushed herself away from the door and walked to the fridge with jerky steps. She was shaking all over, rigid with tension— the shattering effect of seeing him again. Here. And not knowing why.

Business, he'd said. Not the impending divorce? And what had Freda got to do with it? Why should she have written? If she had. But then why should Sebastian lie about a thing like that?

She extracted a carton of eggs with a shaking hand and put it carefully down on the work surface. And behind her, the door swung back on its hinges and Sebastian said in a voice like splintered steel, 'You have a visitor. If I were you, I'd ask him to knock before he walks in next time. When he saw me he looked shattered. I've obviously wrecked his plans for the night. And yours. You should have told me you were expecting your toy boy. I would have gone straight back to Gatwick; I do know how to be discreet.'

CHAPTER TEN

CHARLEY flinched as she met the burning ferocity of Sebastian's eyes, the bitter twist of his mouth. If she hadn't known better she would have accused him of being jealous.

Tearing her eyes from his ravaged face, she walked out of the kitchen, her head held high. How dared he say Gwilym was her toy boy? Because who else would have walked straight in, at this time of night?

Gwilym was standing just inside the front door, rain-water dripping from his hard-worn waxed jacket as he shuffled awkwardly from one booted foot to the other. His eyes lit up briefly as he saw her, but when she asked, none too pleased with him, 'What can I do for you?' he beckoned her over, shaking his head, and Charley knew why, because she could feel the murderous vibes coming from Sebastian from where he stood in the open kitchen doorway.

'Mam sent me up with a message from your aunty,' he explained, his voice barely above a whisper, his eyes on the dark, menacing presence of the man on the other side of the room. 'She'd been trying to get us all afternoon and evening. Only Dad was at the livestock market and Mam and the rest of us went over to visit Gran. She only just got the message to us.'

'She's not ill, is she?' Freda was never ill. But Charley couldn't think of any other reason for her

obviously frantic need to contact her. But Gwilym
shook his head, lowering his voice even further.

'No. She said to warn you Sebastian was on his
way. She hadn't wanted to tell him where you were,
but she had no choice.' His eyes flickered to the far
side of the room and back to Charley. 'It looks like
we were too late. Do you want me to see him off the
premises?'

The spurt of youthful bravado was touching and
stopped Charley laughing in his face. It would take
more than Gwilym to make Sebastian go where he
didn't want to go.

'No, of course not,' she said firmly. She could do
without all this melodrama. Though Freda had had
a point, of course. If she'd been able to get the
message through earlier, then Charley would have
been on her guard, wouldn't have been so shocked by
his unexpected arrival. 'It's business,' she explained,
not altogether too untruthfully. 'And I really don't
mind.' She tried to smile, willing him to go. If she'd
given him the impression that Freda's agitation had
been because she hadn't wanted her niece's holiday
to be broken by a business meeting, that was all to
the good. What was between her and Sebastian was
private and not a subject for endless conjecture in the
farmhouse down the track. 'It breaks the monotony
of a wet evening.'

'Oh, that's all right, then.' His relief was patently
obvious. His offer to throw the Spaniard off the
premises had been made out of misplaced gallantry;
he was probably mightily relieved he wasn't being
called on to carry it through. And his voice was buoy-

antly carrying as he told her, 'I'll get off home, then. Don't forget our date for tomorrow evening.'

He had let himself out before she made any sense of that and remembered his offer to take her to the village hop. She heaved a great sigh and Sebastian grated, 'If you're quick, you can call him back. I'm leaving.' His upper lip lifted in a hateful sneer. 'I wouldn't want to deprive you. When you took up with the fat man I couldn't believe it, but making a lover out of a boy ten years your junior——'

'He's not!' Charley growled at him, her chin going up, wanting to slap him when he came back tersely.

'Two years, ten years—what does it matter?' and walked purposefully towards the door.

He had said he was leaving and he obviously meant it. But not before she had had her say. Who the hell did he think he was?

Quickly she placed herself in front of the door. To get through it he would have to physically move her. And although, five months ago, he had wanted to make love to her, the way he looked now told her he couldn't bear to touch her.

'You're staying until you tell me why you came!' Big amber eyes glittered a challenge into the cold black depths of his. So far as she was aware, no one had ever had the temerity to issue an order to Sebastian Machado before. No one made him do what he didn't want to do, and what he wanted he got. Even Freda had given in.

Her aunt was the strongest-minded woman she knew, yet Sebastian had made her divulge his wife's whereabouts. The apologetic message she'd sent had said she'd had no choice.

Charley could sympathise with her and wondered, shakily, if she could achieve the miracle of making him stay—if only for the few moments necessary to explain his presence here—when he was determined to leave.

She didn't think much of her chances. The look of grim determination on his face, coupled with what had to be naked dislike, told her he'd brush her aside with about the same amount of energy and thought he'd expend on swatting a fly. But not before she'd made him realise he couldn't get away with talking to her like that!

Pressing herself firmly against the door, she lifted her chin and said in a cold little voice, 'Let's get the record straight, just for once. Gwilym—the youngster you were so rude to—is not my lover. And neither was Greg. We planned to marry, but we never made love. I'm not the adulterous partner in our misbegotten marriage. And you still haven't told me why you came.'

He looked at her coolly, 'So I'll write you a letter. Or, better still, get my solicitor to do it for me.'

So it was something to do with the divorce, she thought numbly, gasping raggedly as he took an impatient step forward and clamped his hands on her shoulders, determined to move her out of his way.

Hard fingers bit through the soft fabric of her body-smothering sweatshirt. She could have died! She had never expected to see him again, much less have to endure his touch. And even when he touched her in cold anger she went weak inside with longing. Oh, how she despised herself!

Her eyelids clamped down to hide her self-loathing, then fluttered uncertainly when, far from lifting her aside, his hands were gentling, stroking her shoulders, as if he were discovering her all over again. And she heard him say, his voice rough round the edges, 'So fragile. You have bones like a bird.' His hands slid down to take hers. 'What have you been doing to yourself? Look at me, Charlotte.'

With his fingers twined with hers, what else could she do but obey? Tentatively she raised her lids and watched him through her lashes. He was raking her features with eyes that mirrored concern, and her poor battered heart fluttered inside her breast as he said tightly, 'Freda told me she was worried about you, you were working too hard. She obviously wasn't lying. What are you trying to do? Kill yourself?' He released her hands, but only to run his over her body, the intimacy of his actions making her want to fling herself against him, giving way to the wickedly wanton response only he could draw from her.

But his touch was impersonal, almost clinical. She desperately wanted to cry, and was too busy trying to get back some of her control to answer his, 'You've lost far too much weight. Why is this? Don't tell me you're not happy with your life, Charlotte. After all, you chose it.'

He led her back into the body of the room while she wondered fretfully if it was her perceived lack of weight that had been responsible for the unexpected way he'd changed his mind about leaving. Why should he care? He had finished with her, hadn't he? Washed his hands of her when she'd refused to plunge herself into a loveless marriage all over again.

She was in no state to object as he firmly placed her in one of the armchairs and turned to stoke up the fire. She followed his every movement with huge, over-bright eyes, overwhelmed by all that casual, un-thinking grace of movement. And when he said, 'You mentioned food and coffee. I'll get it. Stay exactly where you are,' she knew she was about to have hys-terics. And there was a shrill and shaming wobble in her voice as she objected,

'I don't want anything. I'm not an invalid, and although I don't claim to be an Einstein, my IQ has got to be higher than minus one!' And at the carefully controlled twitch of his mouth she gathered herself together and said more soberly, 'All I want is to know why you came.' And why you decided to leave in such a hurry after Gwilym appeared, and why you changed your mind again. But she kept those questions firmly to herself. There were too many issues, and all of them murky, without her saying anything to cloud them further.

'I'll tell you while we eat.' He wasn't giving an inch but if he could make stipulations then so could she. She followed him into the kitchen, relieved to find her legs not quite as wobbly as they had been. But then he hadn't touched her for all of five minutes, she derided herself. When he touched her she went haywire; surely she was old enough and sensible enough to cope?

'I am not an invalid,' she repeated in the face of his black frown. 'Besides, you don't know where any-thing is.' It wouldn't take a complete idiot longer than a few minutes to find out. The kitchen was small and compact, everything in its logical place. And she knew why she had followed him in here. She wanted to be near him, to see him, for every minute of the short time remaining. And went pink, because she was such a masochistic fool.

She bustled around, hoping he couldn't read her mind, and gave him the field mushrooms Gwilym had presented her with this morning and asked him to prepare them while she got busy with the egg whisk. And when she felt able, she said with commendable lightness, 'Let's call a truce. It's stupid to fight.' And she didn't look at him in case he was wearing that fiercely proud 'call yourself human?' look of his, just took the plate of neatly chopped mushrooms from him and scooped them into the melted butter in the pan she had ready on the stove. 'How long are you staying in England?'

'I fly back to Jerez tomorrow.'

'But that means . . .' She whipped round. He had found the cutlery and was laying the table. He would have to make the long drive back to Gatwick tonight to be in time to check in for the twice-weekly mid-morning flight to Jerez. And although he had it under control, he couldn't disguise those lines of fatigue. They scored his gorgeous fallen-angel face, making him look older, world-weary. And the weather was still atrocious, the rain driving down as if it would never stop, beating against the windows. 'Can't you delay it?' Loving him, she could no more stop worrying about him that she could stop breathing. 'You've already done too much driving for one day. You should at least get one night's rest before——'

'Are you offering?'

She knew what he meant, and knew from the grim line of his mouth that he expected her to get in a huff, to direct him to the nearest hotel, one that hadn't closed down for the season. And said collectedly, 'Of course. There are two bedrooms. You're welcome to stay overnight.' She turned back to the stove, pouring the beaten eggs over the softened mushrooms, leaving him to make what he liked of her offer, to make up his own mind about whether he accepted it or not.

But he said nothing. She could feel his eyes on her, though. Watching her, making her skin tingle. Biting her bottom lip, she felt the blood course more rapidly through her veins with a betraying throb. Why didn't he say something? Anything. Even if it was only to tell her that he would rather drive to hell and back than spend one more moment than absolutely necessary under this roof with her. He was tearing her nerves to shreds with his dark silence, and her hands were shaking as she divided the omelette between two plates, giving him the lion's share.

As soon as she sat down he swapped the plates, and she looked at the food in front of her and leaned back, closing her eyes as her stomach turned over. She couldn't eat it. How could he expect her to? She heard him ask, 'Did you mean what you said? That spotty youth isn't sharing your bed? In spite of the way he walked in as if he had rights, in spite of the intimate whispered conversation, his reminder of the date you have tomorrow night?'

'He came with a message from Freda,' she replied with a spurt of spirit. 'She wanted to warn me you were on your way. When he saw you he knew he was too late. So he whispered. I don't blame him—the way you were glowering! And he asked me to the village hop because he was sorry for me, I suppose. Only I won't be going.' She pushed her plate away and saw he was eating the much smaller portion with every sign of relish. And for some reason, that made her mad enough to snipe, 'All I can say is you've got a nasty mind!'

'No. An adult one. The spotty youth fancies his chances. It's perfectly obvious. He's at that callow and uncomfortable age when sex is a major preoccupation. And, despite the fact that you've got bones where other women have got something called flesh, you're still an exquisitely desirable woman.' He finished the last of his share of the omelette and laid down his fork. He was almost smiling. 'Strangely enough, I know you're telling the truth when you say you never let Gregory Wilson into your bed. You'd been married to me—you could never have allowed a man like that such intimacies.'

To call him an arrogant, big-headed swine would be stating the obvious. Charley cradled her coffee-cup in both hands. Time to change the subject. Quickly. Before his uncanny ability to find target led him, and her, into much deeper waters.

'You still haven't told me why you came here.'

'Ah.' He turned sideways in his chair, hooking one long, elegantly clad leg over the other, one arm over the back of the chair. His unreadable eyes didn't leave her face. 'Freda wrote. I received the letter just under a week ago. I had a pressing business appointment in Madrid, but as soon as it was dealt with I flew over, arriving, as you know, this morning. I got the details of your whereabouts from your aunt—not without some difficulty. And came down here with a business proposition.'

Charley frowned. 'Why should Freda write to you?' That was what she couldn't understand, and he shrugged.

'So you really don't know? She accused me of neglecting my duty, pointed out that I was a wealthy man and had ruined your life.' Again the minimal shrug, but this time accompanied by a grim twist of his mouth. 'Quite how I ruined it, I fail to understand. I had one year of your life, in marriage. A marriage you walked away from of your own accord because, presumably, you wanted to. Nobody pushed you. You have already admitted that you never believed the things Olivia told you. But be that as it may, Freda said she was worried about you. You were, apparently, working yourself into a state of exhaustion in an attempt to save money towards buying into a partnership with her. She suggested that, since I obviously didn't intend supporting you financially, I should buy back those shares your father owned and left to you.'

'She had no right!' Charley slammed her cup back on its saucer. She would never forgive her aunt for this piece of blatant interference! If she'd wanted to go cap in hand to Sebastian for hand-outs, then she would have done, long ago, would have forced him—through the courts if need be—to support her. 'I don't want anything from you. I never did,' she bit out furiously, and watched his face go stiff with the unforgiving pride that was never far from the surface.

'You've made that clear, more than once. No need to labour the point. Nevertheless, you are entitled to something. I would prefer you to hang on to the shares—it's not a very large block, after all. Their value will increase, of course, and you will continue to receive your annual dividend.'

'So?' Charley bit out, still angry about what her aunt had done, the very finality of this conversation adding to her distress. She had never thought of selling those shares, to him or anyone else. Not until Greg had mentioned it—and gone on mentioning it. And even then she had felt a deep and inexplicable aversion to doing any such thing. She knew now that she had hung on to them because they, and the modest annual dividend, had been her one remaining link with the man she had never stopped loving.

'So what I suggest is this: keep the shares and when the divorce is finalised I will fund your partnership. As I said, you will be entitled. And in the meantime, you needn't worry about saving almost everything you earn. At least you will be able to afford better living accommodation and decent food to eat.'

Wave after wave of black misery engulfed her. She felt too ill to answer. Bleakly, she recognised why, recognised the death of hope. She had been fighting to come to terms with it ever since she had returned from Spain, only to have it resurrected when he had arrived here this evening.

She had tried not to hope, done her level best to squash it. But it must have been there all the time, waiting to hurt and betray her all over again. And now, with his calm, unemotional discussion of divorce, the last, utterly illusory hope had gone.

She stood up, her legs wobbling beneath her, and gathered the plates, stacking them on the draining-board, and from just behind her she heard him say, 'Well?' his voice sharp with impatience.

Turning then, reluctantly, she faced him. His face might have been carved from wood. She dragged in a breath and then shrugged. 'If that's what you want.'

She sounded as if the life had been drained out of her, she knew she did. But surely that couldn't be responsible for the shaft of pure anger that made his eyes look like black coals? Or for the way he grated, 'I'm trying to be civilised about this, to make adequate and proper provision for your future.' His mouth tightened. 'But it is not what I want, and you damn well know it!' One bunched, tight-knuckled hand slammed into the open palm of the other. 'I want you to stay in Cadiz with me, as my wife. I asked you. Twice. And twice you refused. So don't pretend you don't know what I want!'

Charley gulped, her throat constricting. Had he been born to torment her?

Her eyes glittered with unshed tears. The time had come to tie up loose ends. Maybe then he would understand, stop making those bittersweet, torturing suggestions. Earlier she had wondered if it could be the only way out for her, the only way to put the past firmly behind her.

'I can't be your wife. Not if you don't love me. I can't go through that again.'

'What are you talking about?' he asked after a small, still silence.

He sounded weary, as if she bored him, and she could no longer contain the tears. They fell, unchecked, and her head hung forward on her fragile neck and she answered him, her voice sounding shaken and desperate, 'You never loved me. Ever. And I loved you so much. I couldn't bear it. It hurt too much, knowing you didn't care.'

'Ah.'

He sounded as if that explained everything. And it did, of course. He understood now; he would no longer even think of suggesting she stayed married to him. She had won her freedom—of sorts—at the cost of her pride. The pride that had stopped her from telling him the whole truth, the pride that had been the only thing she'd been able to salvage from the wreckage of their marriage.

'What made you think I didn't care!' A surprisingly tender note in his voice, a gentle hand tilting her chin, forced her frightened eyes to open, to look at him. Hooded eyes roamed her face, then he shook his head slowly, his strong fingers tightening fractionally as he asked, his intriguing accent thickening, 'Am I to take it that the only reason you refused my offer of a reconciliation was because you believed I didn't love you, never had loved you?'

She nodded, too choked to speak. She had explained, hadn't she? Did he want his pint of blood as well as his pound of flesh?

'There is nothing to cry about, little pigeon.' Surprisingly, his eyes were smiling, glinting wickedly, just as she remembered them. Her heart twisted inside her with bittersweet, loving pain. And his mouth was curved in that effortlessly sensual, sinfully charming way that was his alone, transforming those autocratically handsome features into a thing of glory. He was gorgeous—it was just too much to bear!

Then the sob in her throat relaxed and melted away as he feathered her tear-stained cheeks with the balls of his thumbs and repeated, 'No need for tears. You love me. All is well.'

She gave him a watery smile, her heart breaking. Oh, how she loved him! And he knew it, and had no compunction about letting her know he knew it. In another man she would have called it conceit. But with Sebastian it was simply a glorious self-assurance. Just as he had told her, back in Cadiz, that he had never seen Greg as a problem simply because, having been married to him, she would never be able to put such an inferior being in his place! Just as he was now telling her that, having loved him once, she would never be able to stop.

Which was, unfortunately, true.

And now there was nothing left to say.

She stepped back, away from his weakening touch, with nothing to say except, 'I'll think about your offer to buy me the partnership in Freda's agency.'

She found herself taken in two inescapable hands, forced back against the hard warmth of his body, heard him scorn, 'You will not. The offer is withdrawn. Now I know why you continually rejected me, everything is simple. You will return to Cadiz with me, as my wife. Where I go, you will go. You will never leave me again.'

He was covering her face with tiny kisses and she felt her body melt into his, and before she could blindly give in to all he asked of her she said desperately, 'But nothing has changed! I won't go through all that pain——'

'No,' he agreed severely. 'Nothing has changed, and it never will. I have always loved you, above all else.'

Her heart gave a great, bounding leap of excitement, and as his mouth ravaged hers in a fiercely possessive kiss she wondered if she dared believe him, and was almost beyond caring whether she could or not when he thrust her away for a second, his magnificent eyes blazing as he fought for control, found it, then picked her up in his arms and carried her through to the other room and sank down into an armchair, cradling her on his lap.

'And now,' he instructed softly, 'tell me why I married such an idiot. Tell me why you think I should marry a woman I didn't love.'

Put like that, she did come over as a prize idiot. She smiled softly, savouring the magic of the moment, just this moment, burrowing her face against the fabric of his suit jacket, hearing the steady, strong beats of his heart.

There was only this one blissful moment for her, a fragment of time when she could allow herself to believe him, believe he had married her for love, and loved her still.

Then, regretfully, she pushed herself upright, felt his hands tighten around her waist, and was caught in the honeyed trap of his arms. Dredging up the courage she needed to remind him of that dreadful woman, she flicked the tip of her tongue over her lips and choked out, 'Olivia told me the truth. That day. You were away. She came to me and told me that you and she had been lovers for years, that you would have been married long ago, but she wouldn't agree because she was unable to have children—an accident in childhood, she said. She knew you wanted an heir. It was important to you.'

Her voice faltered. Sebastian had gone very still. She could feel the tension coiling through his body, transmitting itself to hers. She was beginning to shiver, fine tremors that shook her whole body.

'And then you decided to marry me,' she went on stoically, hating what she was having to say, dreading the outcome, his stark admission of the truth of it. 'You chose to have a civil wedding ceremony, because then you would be able to divorce me once I'd provided you with an heir. But we hadn't had a child; there was no sign of one. Olivia said you were getting impatient, sick of me and the whole set-up. She was warning me.'

His very silence, his utter stillness, should have led her to expect the worst, but she was so bound up within the painful memories that she was totally unprepared for his explosion of fury, the way he jack-knifed to his feet, spilling her off his lap, only saved from falling in an ignominious heap on the hearth rug by a cruel hand that snatched her arm and hauled her on to her feet.

'Warning you! *Dios*! And you believed her? Above me—your husband? Am I to be put through this torment once again? *Dios*—I wash my hands of you!'

He bunched his fists into his trouser pockets, pacing the floor in a fury, his shoulders high and wide, pride flaring through his rage-pale nostrils. Charley shuddered, not knowing what to say. She hadn't expected this reaction and didn't know how to deal with it.

'You mean it wasn't true?' she croaked, and watched him go still, stiffen, then twist round on his heels, his black eyes impaling her.

'And would you believe me if I said it wasn't?' he derided austerely. 'Would you take my word against that of a lying, conniving, neurotic bitch?' His mouth twisted in blistering condemnation. 'Or would trusting your husband be asking too much? You were quick enough to tell me how thoroughly you believed her when she lied about my role in Fernando's death. Quick enough to run away and accuse me of murder! Do you know how much that hurt? Do you?'

He looked savage enough to tear her into little pieces, and the silence was terrible. Even the wind and rain had stopped pounding the cottage. She bit down on her lip, understanding how he must have felt, and made her voice calm as she reminded him, 'I never really believed that part of it. When I stopped to think, later, when I'd recovered from the initial trauma of being told you'd only married me to use me, I knew you weren't capable of killing your own brother in cold blood. I've already apologised. What else can I do?'

'You can tell me what stopped you hurling the other accusation at me,' he said in a cold, hating voice. 'You mumbled something about my being welcome to her, about her having been my mistress—but I disregarded it, put it down to childish spite. So enlighten me,' he demanded, folding his arms across his chest and giving her a cutting, bristling glare.

'Pride,' she answered simply, refusing to be the first to look away. 'I've already told you that when I calmed down enough to begin to think straight I couldn't believe you'd killed Fernando. But the other—that was something I couldn't come to terms with...hearing Olivia tell me that you and she were lovers, that she regarded me as no threat because I was just a stupid teenager, vapid and plain, and would be given my marching orders after I'd provided you with an heir. I couldn't tell you. It would have reminded you of what I was—a clinging, besotted, lovelorn nobody, willing to lick your boots for the small reward of your fleeting notice. Pride was all I had left. I had nothing else.'

The blaze in his eyes intensified, a deep frown indenting his brow before, just briefly, he covered his face with his hands, slowing dragging them away, saying in a stricken voice, 'Pride! I was born with it. God knows, I can understand it in you. Such a sin!' He reached for her with a groan, pulling her into his arms, his head against hers, his voice muffled and thick as he muttered emotionally, 'God forgive us both!' He lifted his head and looked deeply into her eyes. She saw the shimmer of tears in the black depths and reached up, kissing him in anguish. And for a moment he responded, then gently withdrew, cupping her face in warm, strong hands.

'Pride was what kept me from coming to claim you back,' he admitted thickly. 'It wouldn't let me forgive you for believing what that bitch had said about my part in my brother's death instead of trusting me, your husband. But still you tortured me. You were never out of my thoughts. I had you watched, your every movement reported back. I told myself I was biding my time, waiting for the opportunity for revenge, to make you feel the kind of pain you had given me. In reality...' He brushed his lips over her eyelids and tears brimmed. He stroked them away with his fingers. 'In reality, I knew I couldn't bear to lose sight of you; I couldn't stop hoping. At the end of each day I wondered if the next would bring you back to me. I kept fresh white roses in your room, waiting for you, just as I was waiting for you, too proud to come to you and beg.'

'Oh, Sebastian!' she groaned dazedly. 'You do love me!'

'Since I first saw you.' He kissed the tip of her nose, holding her tenderly, as if she might break. 'You were so young, so vulnerable, so innocent. So beautiful. My heart was instantly yours. You had suffered a terrible bereavement and were being badgered by that harridan of an aunt. I wanted to take you away with me there and then—care for you, love you, keep you safe, watch you blossom. Is it any wonder I married you in one big hurry?'

His cheek rasped against hers. He needed a shave. She gloried in the sensation, squirming against him. She heard the ragged intake of his breath and nearly went wild, frowning as he told her soberly, 'But loving you brought its problems. You were so young— younger than your years. So innocent. And my passion was so great. I was afraid of hurting you, or frightening you. And so I insisted on separate rooms, on limiting my nights with you. I was waiting for you to grow up, recognise your sexuality.'

'And all the time I was afraid of being inadequate. I was sure you rarely came to my room because you were disappointed in me, and sure you spent all your time working because I bored you.'

'You never bored me, *querida*!' he murmured against her lips. 'At that time I still had to work hard. Under Fernando's direction the business had gone rapidly downhill. I was building it up. For us. I should have explained. I thought you were happy—how could I have known you were not? You should have told me.'

'I was too insecure,' she admitted shakily. 'That's why I was able to believe Olivia when she said you were lovers.' She dropped her head against his shoulder, willing him to understand. 'And when I spoke to you on the phone that day, I was distraught. I told you I was leaving you, and why. All I needed was for you to say it was all a pack of lies. I would have believed you. Just one word, and I would have come back on the next flight. But you said nothing. You didn't deny a single thing. I thought then it was because you couldn't, because it was true.'

He cupped her face with strong hands, his eyes anguished as they held hers, his voice husky as he regretted, 'It was this damnable pride, *cariña*. You must understand—you have your share, after all. When you made those accusations you put me in a state of shock. Then pride took over. I shouldn't have to tell you that nothing of what you'd heard was the truth, not a single word. I shouldn't have to beg. You were my loved wife; you should have trusted me implicitly. That was what my pride told me. It was pride that made me let you believe what you would, pride that kept me from you for four agonising years.' He pulled her roughly into his arms. 'How could I have known you felt so threatened, so insecure? As far as I was concerned, you were my beautiful, gentle

Charlotte, my wife. You had a permanent, unassailable place in my heart while Olivia was simply a valued employee.'

'But she seemed to be everything I was not,' she confessed shakily. 'She was intelligent, beautiful, charming. Slim. When she came to Cadiz, which was often, she was with you all the time while I was left at home, doing the flowers, wondering what I could do to make you notice me the way you noticed her. And I believed I was everything she said I was: barely out of my teens and young for my age. Inexperienced, plain and fat.'

'How silly you still are, my love! When you admitted to me that you had never truly believed me capable of murder I was so sure that you had also discounted what that dreadful woman had said about our so-called affair. I didn't know, because you hadn't told me, the whole of the story. When you sent the fat man back to England I was even more convinced. Especially as you responded so beautifully to my loving. That is why I was so bitter when you refused to stay with me. Oh, Charlotte, you must know I would love you, find you beautiful, whether you are nineteen or ninety, thin as a pin or large as a house!'

He put her away from him, but gently. Removing the jacket of his beautifully cut suit, he tossed it carelessly on to a chair and marched into the kitchen, dragging her behind him. 'I will make coffee, and I will speak of that unspeakable woman. For the last time. You understand?'

He gave her a fierce look, tinged with the pride she adored. She didn't want to talk about that woman either, but was content to listen to whatever he felt he had to say. He loved her; that was the only important thing in her world.

'She had to be insane,' he told her as he gushed water into the kettle and crashed about in the cupboard where the mugs were kept. 'However, I was not aware of that to begin with.' His lofty tone made Charley's mouth twitch, and he tilted his head suspiciously before giving her a radiant, forgiving smile. 'She'd had an affair with Fernando, but that didn't surprise me. He was unable to resist any attractive female who crossed his path. And she, of course, had crossed his path over the streamlining of the UK import branch. After his death she turned her attentions to me. I didn't encourage her. She wasn't my type—too brittle, too obvious. But she was excellent at her job—a little too demanding of my time when she visited Head Office, but then she often had extremely innovative ideas which could benefit the company. And so I pretended not to notice her interest; she was a valuable employee and I can be obtuse, if it suits me.'

The coffee made, he put the two mugs on the table and took the chair opposite, his face serious as he covered her hand with his.

'What I was slow to understand was the depth and depravity of her obsession with me. In her mind, she saw me as belonging to her. And so I didn't even consider that she might be jealous to the point of insanity when I fell in love for the first time and married you before you could change your mind. So she made up that pack of lies to frighten what she saw as the opposition away.'

'What happened to her?' Charley couldn't help asking, and his eyes blazed briefly.

'What do you think? When I learned of her evil lies, from you, I fired her on the spot. I threatened to sue her for defamation of character, for slander, to throw the book at her if she ever showed her face around me or mine again. She was still at my home when I returned from that business trip. You phoned from England. And after that call I left the office to find her. She was in my bed.' At the look of anguish that peaked Charley's face, his grip tightened on her hand. 'She was not invited. She put herself there. I threw her out. And fired her. And talking of beds...' He stood up, his coffee barely touched. 'Didn't you say something about offering me one for the night?'

She went limpidly into his arms, and was scarcely aware of how they got upstairs. But they were in her room and he kicked off his shoes and threw himself down on the bed, on his back, his arms crossed behind his head, his eyes wicked as he commanded, 'Undress me...'

She came awake to the sound of birdsong and the feather-light caress of his lips against the curve of her naked shoulder. She made a mewing sound of pleasure in her throat and remembered, as if in a dream, how the last of her reservations had been swept aside at one point during the night.

Drowsy from lovemaking, she had nestled up against him, her voice blurry as she'd asked, 'Remember the day in the hills? You asked me to stay on, as your wife. And I asked you if it was for the sake of having children, and you said, "What else?" '

She had felt him nod, felt his fingers idle through her hair, drawing her head deeper into the curve of his shoulder.

'Why did you say that?' she prodded. If he hadn't, she probably wouldn't have left and pride wouldn't have kept them apart for these extra five long months.

'I thought it was what you wanted to hear.' There was a smile in his voice. 'It had nothing whatsoever to do with my supposedly evil plans to get a child of my body on you and then turn you out into the snow. About six months into our marriage you said you wanted a child. Or don't you remember? You seemed very anxious to conceive at this time.'

So she had, she recalled with a jolt of understanding. At the time she had believed a child would bring them closer together, not knowing that it was her own immaturity, the sense of insecurity Olivia had given her, that was keeping them apart.

She smiled softly into the darkness, her hand wandering, and Sebastian said thickly, 'What are you doing?'

'What do you think...?'

Now she stirred gently, blissfully content, then spun out of control as his hand cupped her breast beneath the covers.

Last night he had commanded her to undress him but it had ended by them undressing each other in a tangle of eager limbs and demanding kisses. Until the intensity of desire had become unbearable and he had ordered thickly, 'Tell me you love me!'

And she had, time and time again, with each possessive, ecstasy-giving thrust of his passionate body, each giving, each taking, soaring into a world o blinding light, and magic—the inexplicable, never-ending magic of love.

And now, as he turned her on to her back, his wicked black eyes gleamed into hers as he murmured, 'My passion doesn't alarm you, *querida*?'

'I think I might manage to live with it,' she answered huskily, twining her arms around his neck, drawing his head down to her parted lips. She could feel the magnificence of his arousal, and her flesh quivered as he parted her legs with a nudge of his thigh, and her body opened to him, flowered for him, all her love in her eyes.

And later, much later, as she heard him whistling in the shower, she rolled languidly out of bed, a little-cat smile on her passion-bruised lips as she belted her robe around her waist and padded down to the kitchen to make tea. Then wandered back through the living-room when she heard Gwilym's knock.

He was, as ever, burdened down with a carton of goodies from his mam. His eyes widened as he took in her state of undress, her tousled hair and dreamy eyes. And behind her, Sebastian said, 'Not today, thank you,' in that 'Do you call yourself human?' tone of voice, and Charley suppressed the desire to giggle helplessly and said kindly,

'It's very good of your mother, Gwilym. But we're a bit overstocked as it is. And my husband and I will be making tracks back to Cadiz today or tomorrow. I'll call by before we leave and thank you all properly for all your help.' And she closed the door quietly on his shell-shocked face, and Sebastian wrapped his arms around her, nuzzling the back of her neck.

'Today I feel generous enough to be sorry for him. He lusted after the most desirable woman in the world, only to find I have taken her.'

His hands slid up to stroke her breasts and she gasped, turning in his arms. All he was wearing was a tiny towel, and she told him breathily, 'The kettle's on for tea.'

'Good.' He dragged open her robe and nestled her against him, skin to skin. 'We'll go back home tomorrow. You can write your aunt a letter. Or phone her from the airport.' His towel fell to the floor, and Charley gasped all over again and wriggled closer. 'Today I need to rest, remember? You were the one to insist that I have a night's rest before driving to the airport. But I had no rest at all, which is your fault, of course! But first I will make tea. And toast. Keep the bed warm for me.'

'You'll catch your death like that!' she gurgled, loving his arrogant bearing as he strode, mother-naked, through to the kitchen. But he simply gave her that devilish grin, over his shoulder.

'Then you will have the job of warming me up, little pigeon. I think I shall enjoy it. It is worth being in this cold and damp country for that pleasure alone. Go, keep the sheets warm for me!'

So she went, boneless as she was. And she would see he did get the rest he needed. She would do all the work in bed today. And that was the promise her eyes gave him as he joined her minutes later. A promise she kept, revelling in her love for him and his for her, the future unclouded, belonging to them both.

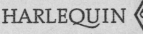

Fifty red-blooded, white-hot, true-blue hunks
from every State in the Union!

Look for MEN MADE IN AMERICA! Written by some
of our most popular authors, these stories feature some
of the strongest, sexiest men, each from a different state
in the union!

Two titles available every month at your favorite
retail outlet.

In January, look for:

WITHIN REACH by Marilyn Pappano (New Mexico)
IN GOOD FAITH by Judith McWilliams (New York)

In February, look for:

THE SECURITY MAN by Dixie Browning
(North Carolina)
A CLASS ACT by Kathleen Eagle
(North Dakota)

You won't be able to resist MEN MADE IN AMERICA!

HARLEQUIN®

PRESENTS *Plus*

It wasn't the best start to a working relationship:
Debra's private detective sister had asked her to spy on
Marsh Graham—Debra's new boss! But if Debra began
by believing Marsh had suspicious motives, she soon
realized that, when it came to her, Marsh had desires of
a more personal kind....

Was Denzil Black moving from woman to woman, seduc-
ing them, then leaving them drained and helpless? Clare
thought of Denzil as a vampire lover...so when she realized that she was next on his list of conquests, she re-
solved that *Denzil* would learn what it was to be a victim of love!

In Presents Plus, there's more to love....

Watch for:

A Matter of Trust by Penny Jordan
Harlequin Presents Plus #1719

and

Vampire Lover by Charlotte Lamb
Harlequin Presents Plus #1720

Harlequin Presents Plus
The best has just gotten better!

Available in February, wherever Harlequin books are sold.

On the most romantic day of the year, capture the thrill of falling in love all over again—with

Harlequin's

Bachelors

They're three sexy and *very single* men who run very special personal ads to find the women of their fantasies by Valentine's Day. These exciting, passion-filled stories are written by bestselling Harlequin authors.

Your Heart's Desire by Elise Title
Mr. Romance by Pamela Bauer
Sleepless in St. Louis by Tiffany White

Be sure not to miss Harlequin's Valentine Bachelors, available in February wherever Harlequin books are sold.

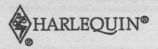

HARLEQUIN®

Don't miss these Harlequin favorites by some of our most distinguished authors!
And now, you can receive a discount by ordering two or more titles!

HT#25577	WILD LIKE THE WIND by Janice Kaiser	$2.99	☐
HT#25589	THE RETURN OF CAINE O'HALLORAN by JoAnn Ross	$2.99	☐
HP#11626	THE SEDUCTION STAKES by Lindsay Armstrong	$2.99	☐
HP#11647	GIVE A MAN A BAD NAME by Roberta Leigh	$2.99	☐
HR#03293	THE MAN WHO CAME FOR CHRISTMAS by Bethany Campbell	$2.89	☐
HR#03308	RELATIVE VALUES by Jessica Steele	$2.89	☐
SR#70589	CANDY KISSES by Muriel Jensen	$3.50	☐
SR#70598	WEDDING INVITATION by Marisa Carroll	$3.50 U.S. $3.99 CAN.	☐
HI#22230	CACHE POOR by Margaret St. George	$2.99	☐
HAR#16515	NO ROOM AT THE INN by Linda Randall Wisdom	$3.50	☐
HAR#16520	THE ADVENTURESS by M.J. Rodgers	$3.50	☐
HS#28795	PIECES OF SKY by Marianne Willman	$3.99	☐
HS#28824	A WARRIOR'S WAY by Margaret Moore	$3.99 U.S. $4.50 CAN.	☐

(limited quantities available on certain titles)

	AMOUNT	$
DEDUCT:	10% DISCOUNT FOR 2+ BOOKS	$
ADD:	POSTAGE & HANDLING	$
	($1.00 for one book, 50¢ for each additional)	
	APPLICABLE TAXES*	$_____
	TOTAL PAYABLE	$_____
	(check or money order—please do not send cash)	

To order, complete this form and send it, along with a check or money order for the total above, payable to Harlequin Books, to: **In the U.S.:** 3010 Walden Avenue, P.O. Box 9047, Buffalo, NY 14269-9047; **In Canada:** P.O. Box 613, Fort Erie, Ontario, L2A 5X3.

Name: _____

Address: _____ City: _____

State/Prov.: _____ Zip/Postal Code: _____

*New York residents remit applicable sales taxes.
 Canadian residents remit applicable GST and provincial taxes.

HBACK-JM2